D0952178

The Journal of C.J. Jackson

A Dust Bowl Migrant

BY WILLIAM DURBIN

Scholastic Inc. New York

Oklahoma
1935

April 7, 1935, Cimarron County, Oklahoma

If anybody ever tells you that a rattlesnake always rattles before it bites, don't you believe them. I know 'cause one got me this very afternoon.

Mother asked me to fetch some water, so I grabbed two pails and marched down to the windmill. As I reached for the door of our well house, I was thinking how dumb it was of me to have missed *disaster* on my spelling test. I've seen that word a hundred times in the *Boise City News,* describing what it's been like for us farmers in the Oklahoma Panhandle since we got hit with the double whammy of the drought and the Depression.

That's when I saw the rattler only a few inches from the toe of my boot. I jumped backward and landed smack on top of a second snake. He drilled me in the middle of my calf.

Dancing like I'd latched onto the business end of a branding iron, I shook loose from the snake and ran back to the house lickety-split. My heart was hammering so hard that I could barely swallow. I yelled for Daddy, who was working on our Model T truck down by the barn. He walked up to the house at his normal slow gait and looked at me funny until I stammered, "I'm snake bit."

"Where?" was all he said. I pointed to the back of my leg, and he went right to work. He sat me down on the steps and pulled up my pant leg. I twisted my head around until I could see the fang marks. The skin around the two little holes was red and puffy, and my calf felt hot.

Mother had heard the commotion by then. She opened the back door to see what was wrong. "A snake got C.J.," Daddy said calmly. "You'd better get us a chicken."

Mother lit out for the chicken coop. I'd never seen her run so fast. While Daddy was waiting for her to get back, he flicked open the sharpest blade on his jackknife. He told me to lie still, but I turned to get a look at what he was doing. As he cut between the fang marks, I only felt a little prick. Then Daddy grabbed ahold of my leg and squeezed the cut between his big, calloused thumbs. He pumped it slow and steady. "We'll milk her good while we're waiting for the chicken, C.J."

Then Daddy called for my sister Olive. Though Olive is only eleven and real excitable, Daddy never gave her a chance to get upset. The minute she stuck her head out the door, he told her to call Doc Hall and then collect some clean strips of cloth. Olive is a grand talker who loves to ask questions, but Daddy told her to scoot and do what he said. About that time Grandpa woke up from his nap and came to see what the ruckus was about. He took one look and said he would make sure Olive got through to the Doc.

By the time Mother got back with the chicken, my little brothers, Lester and Dalton, and my baby sister, Belle, had come outside to watch Daddy work me over. As soon as Olive brought the strips of cloth, Daddy looked at Mother and said, "Let's do her."

Quick as a lick he grabbed that chicken by both legs and split it down the middle with his knife. Before the guts could spill out, he strapped that poor dying bird onto the back of my leg. My brothers just stared, but little Belle buried her face in Olive's dress and wouldn't look up no more.

April 8

I suffered something awful yesterday. Daddy made me wear that bloody chicken tied around my leg the whole time we were waiting for Doc Hall to drive out here from Boise City. Once the bird's heart stopped beating, I figured Daddy would let me take it off, but he said we needed to make sure all the poison was drawed out. I looked at Mother, but she shook her head and said, "You best wait, C.J."

Daddy is lucky that Mother always takes his side, because you'd have to travel a far piece to find a woman more stubborn. Once she makes up her mind, there is no sense wasting your breath arguing. Daddy smiles when she gets that way — "planting her feet firm" is what he calls it. He says that's the Cherokee side of her coming out. At a glance you hardly notice that my mother is half Cherokee, but the longer you study her, the more her native beauty shines through. Though most of the ladies in these parts pin their hair up, Mother lets hers hang loose. Her hair is shiny black like her eyes, and she stands straight and tall, even though it puts her dead level with Daddy, who's more of a sloucher.

When Doc Hall pulled up in his little Ford coupe, his gray beard had blown off to one side like it always does when he drives fast. "How you all doin'?" he said, swinging his bag in his hand and trying to relax everyone with a big smile. Then he added, "So where's the boy who's been wrasslin' rattlesnakes?" Being in no mood for teasing, I told him it was me and asked when I could take the bloody chicken off my leg. He scolded me for fretting. "This little pullet may have saved your life, Charles

Jefferson Jackson." Then he joked, "That's as good a use of a leghorn as a Sunday dinner, ain't it?"

I didn't care one bit for his joking, and I let him know it. I've seen a diamondback rattlesnake drop a ground squirrel dead in a quivering minute, and at that moment I had severe doubts about whether I would live to see suppertime.

After the doctor cleaned my wound and checked me over, he pronounced me fit as a fiddle. That was hard for me to believe, since my leg hurt like someone was driving hot pins into it. The doctor said that my heavy overalls and my shaking the snake loose so quick are what saved me. Then he tried for one last laugh by telling me that I would live long enough to wear out many rocking chairs. I made it a point not to show even a hint of a smile.

Later

Doc told me to "take it easy" for a few days. To Mother that means flat-out bed rest. Now that I'm stuck in bed, I'm glad I've got this journal to keep me company. It was a birthday present from my aunt Ruby last month. Ruby is my favorite aunt. She has a radio and always invites us over to listen to our favorite shows like *Amos 'n' Andy* and *The Lone Ranger*. We never miss President Roosevelt's fireside chats either. I still remember the speech where he told us that no matter how rough the Depression gets, the only thing we need to be afraid of is fear itself. (He should have added rattlers, too!)

I thanked Ruby for the journal that day, but on the way home I complained to Mother that I wouldn't have anything to write about because nothing ever happened to me. The next thing you know, I'm snake bit!

Though I've barely fevered up at all, the skin around my bite is an angry red color with streaks of yellow and purple mixed in. And it still burns like the devil. Thankfully my leg hasn't swelled up too bad. A rancher was bit over by Wheeless last summer, and his leg got so big they had to cut his pants off.

Evening

Mother has sentenced me to one more day of rest. She's propped up my back and shoulders so any leftover poison can't flow toward my heart, and she's making me drink so much water that my eyeballs are floating.

April 9

I'm sitting on the back porch writing in my journal this morning. Mother said I could rest out here as long as I kept my leg up on a milk stool. I told her I was feeling fine, but she said, "You get your leg up or get back to bed."

Since another duster is kicking up, I expect she'll let me help her take the wash in. The younguns, Dalton and Belle, who have just turned five and four, are way too short to reach the clothesline, and Olive and Lester are at school. In our county we say "the land is on fire" when the soil starts lifting into the air, and by the looks of the sky, we're in for a good blow. If we don't hurry, Mother will have to wash everything all over again.

I'll finish this later.

April 10

I never had a chance to write any more yesterday. The duster got so bad that we had to go through our regular dust storm routine. We locked the cows in the barn, turned the washtubs over and weighted them down, and tied the windmill off. There was no need to shoo the chickens into the henhouse because the dark sky had tricked them into thinking it was time to roost.

By noon the storm was so bad that Daddy drove over to the school and picked up Olive and Lester. Daddy guessed the wind hit forty miles per hour and held right there. As the steady, straight-line blow ripped across the prairie, the dust rose into the sky and everything turned yellow-gray. Soon the air got so thick that I couldn't even see from the house to the barn. All we could do was check our sealing tape, hang wet sheets over the doors and windows, and wait out the storm.

The dust has been blowing bad for several years in a row now. And with the crop failures coming back-to-back like they have, hundreds of families have lost their farms. A Monday never passes without Sheriff Jake Allison posting a notice of a foreclosure at the Boise City courthouse. Times are so rough that when they hold an auction to sell a place, the only people who show up are the banks and the insurance companies. Nobody else has a nickel.

Daddy says the banks own more land than all the farmers and ranchers put together. We are lucky that our place is mortgage-free. Daddy was smart not to buy a bunch of equipment on credit like so many of our neighbors did. Everyone figured that getting rich in the wheat market was a sure thing. They bought big McCormick-Deering tractors and one-way disk plows and got so far in debt they needed to bring in a cash crop every single year to make their payments. Once the drought hit they lost their machinery. Next they lost their farms. We used to have at least forty families living in the townships between Beaver Creek and Boise City. Now all but a handful have left. Our four-horse team can't plow as much ground as a tractor, but the bank isn't waiting to repossess those horses the minute our crops fail. Daddy just plain likes horses, too. He agrees with the famous Oklahoma comedian Will Rogers, who says, "There is something the matter with a man that don't love a horse."

The crop failures have gotten worse every year. An article in the newspaper reported that Cimarron County wheat brought in a whopping $700,000 in 1930. (I turned eight that year, and I will never forget the fine birthday parties that Olive and I had.) But by 1933 the countywide yield was down to a measly $7,000. The real kicker was last year, though. The sum total profit from wheat farming in Cimarron County was $0.

Last fall the farmers did their best to make up for those bad years by busting out all the new land they could. Many, my family included, have invested their last pennies in seed. That scares Daddy a lot. Not only is this going to be what he calls a "make or break" year, but with all that new land plowed up, if the rains don't come, a big storm could blow out the whole Panhandle.

April 12

Daddy heard that last Wednesday's duster was so bad down at the Amarillo airport that a pilot was blinded by a dust cloud at 15,000 feet. I worry that the dust might damage Lester or Belle's lungs. Though most of us Jacksons are rugged stock, Lester and Belle have always been pale and skinny. They take sick real easy, and lately they've both had rattly coughs.

Thousands of birds and jackrabbits suffocated during the storm, and their bodies are lying all over. Dalton and Belle felt sorry for the half-dozen critters that died near our place, and they scooped out shallow graves behind the barn for them.

I can't get used to how gray and wasted everything looks. Before the drought, crops used to grow like all get-out here on the prairie. When I was a little boy, folks raised sorghum and maize and broomcorn. The cattle got fat, and the standing wheat stretched as far as you could see. The untilled ground waved with buffalo grass and wildflowers. Then came the dust and the wind.

These days we run cattle on the largest part of our land and plant the rest with wheat and dryland corn for hog feed. The price of beef drops every year, and our wheat yield hasn't paid for seed costs. The only things that grow worth a darn are nettles and Russian thistles.

Our family spending money comes from the cash we get helping Mother sell eggs and cream in town. We couldn't survive without our garden, which we all help weed and water, and Mother's jackrabbit stew.

April 13

Daddy has asked me twice this evening if I felt strong enough to go to the funeral tomorrow. They are burying an old preacher named William Guy over in Kenton. He was one of the first settlers in the Panhandle and a good friend of our family, so it is only right that I go.

Mother is still keeping a close eye on me. She touches my forehead all the time to make sure I'm not fevering up, and twice each day she swabs smelly Mercurochrome on my fang marks to make sure they don't get infected. Even Daddy, who hates spending time indoors, has been checking up on me a lot lately. He surprised me by buying me a Zane Grey book in town this morning. It's called *Desert Gold*. I've been a great fan of Mr. Grey's ever since I read *Riders of the Purple Sage*. Being that Daddy is usually not much of a talker, all his visiting is very unusual. I have a suspicion that he thought the snakebite had done me in. After watching Grandma die last October, I think he's taken about all the dying he can stand.

Though my daddy is a tight-lipped fellow, he is a very hard worker and is well respected by the folks here in Cimarron County. He's a tall, lanky man who's not yet forty, but his hair has thinned out and gone mostly gray. Whipcord strong, he can wrassle down a calf or pound a fence post home without even breaking into a sweat. Daddy's not mean, but he's got a powder flash temper. His square chin and deep-set gray eyes show that he's not the sort to give up.

I'd better quit writing now so I can help Mother carry water. I'll keep my eyes peeled when I get near our well house.

Later

The Mitchells stopped by to say they were leaving for Arizona. Lester feels real bad 'cause he and Sam Mitchell have been friends since the first grade.

Every time one of our neighbors pulls up stakes and moves, Daddy says, "We got to try our best to hang on." And hang on we do. When we can't afford coal for our stove, we gather cow chips. When feed is hard to come by for the cattle, we chop up soap weed and burn the spines off cactus. And when we don't have any hogs to butcher, we eat what Daddy calls "Hoover hogs," another name for jackrabbits. I can't figure out how every other critter on the plains is struggling to survive the drought — even the birds look parched and dusty — yet rabbits have overrun our whole county.

Daddy gets his grit from Grandma and Grandpa. They were tough folks who homesteaded on the Panhandle in 1907, just as Oklahoma was becoming a state. Before statehood they called this country No Man's Land because none of the surrounding states wanted to claim it. Grandma and Grandpa told me lots of stories about the old days. They were both born in Ohio, or "O-hi," as Grandma liked to call it. Grandma was only fifteen years old when she married Grandpa. He was considerable older and had spent most of his life working in a coal mine. A doctor said he'd got black lung from the coal dust and recommended that he move to a place where the air was clear and dry. They headed west in a mule wagon. Grandma was only seventeen, but she already had two younguns, my daddy and his big brother, Grant.

After tenant farming in Missouri for a few years, they ran across a fancy brochure advertising land for sale in Boise City, Oklahoma. The pictures showed lakes and streams and trees and shady streets. So they scraped all their nickels together and set out for Cimarron County. They arrived to find one strip of sidewalk, a concrete-block house, and a windmill in the open plot of ground that had been set aside to build a courthouse. Otherwise there wasn't nothing but empty prairie in every direction you looked. (The three men who printed up those brochures made thousands of dollars selling worthless lots before the law put them in the penitentiary like they deserved.)

April 14

Though Mother still insists on checking my leg every day, it feels as good as new. We just got home from church. Mother and Olive sang a duet and did a real nice job. It always amazes me how Mother is so shy that she won't hardly ever speak in front of a group, yet she just loves to sing. Mother always looks nervous to begin with, but as soon as she hits the first note, a confident smile stretches across her face. Everybody perks up and listens, too. Daddy says her voice reminds him of a clear spring morning. Olive, on the other hand, doesn't have a natural voice like Mother, yet she practices every chance she gets because her dream is to become "a star of the stage and silver screen."

After a week of small dust storms, the sky has turned bright blue, and the birds are flitting around the barn and fence lines like they should in April. Daddy says it's time to head on up to Kenton for William Guy's funeral.

I was just thinking that for a boy who claimed he didn't have nothing to write about, I sure am filling in the pages of this journal. But when I tell one thing it seems to lead to another.

April 15

Though it's already dark outside and I shouldn't be wasting the lamp oil, I want to write down everything that happened yesterday while it's still clear in my mind.

By the time we got ready to leave, it had turned hot for the first time all year. Though we were fixing to go to a funeral, it was hard not to enjoy the summery scent in the air. Even Daddy, who is generally all business, had a hint of a smile on his face.

We started out for Kenton after lunch. Our '27 Model T Ford truck was crowded. The adults rode inside the cab while we kids sat in the pickup box. Our truck is Daddy's pride and joy. He ordered it brand new as a "knocked down" model, meaning the parts came in a railroad crate, and he put it together himself. He used to keep it polished inside and out, but lately he's happy just to keep it running. He says the truck is getting "tired" because like all the engines in these parts, dust has got inside the crankcase and worn down the piston rings and cylinder walls.

On our way up Highway 64 we crossed the Santa Fe Trail, one of the main routes that took travelers west in the early days. We also passed not too far from Autograph Rock, a sandstone cliff that's chiseled with the names of hundreds of pioneers.

Kenton lies in a quiet valley in the foothills of the Black Mesa. We used to go on hikes and picnics up there when we could afford the gas. Black Mesa doesn't look like much from a distance, but as you get closer, it jumps right into the sky. There's three spines of red and black rock that we call Piney Mountain and "Old Maid," a rock formation that gives a perfect side view of a lady's face. "Wedding Party" shows a minister, bride, and groom. But the best thing about the whole place is dinosaur bones. After a rainstorm, which isn't very likely, or a big wind, bones are lying right on top of the ground. Not long ago a professor from Oklahoma City dug up a brontosaurus leg bone that was six feet long and two feet around!

There was a big turnout for the funeral. Cars and horses and wagons pulled in from as far away as Elkhart and Texhoma. During the graveside service the air was hot and still. As the speeches wore on, I began to notice that an unnatural quiet had settled over the valley.

A short while later a big flock of birds passed overhead. Then a second flock landed at the edge of the cemetery fence. The birds were fluttering around like they'd seen the shadow of a hawk, but the sky was empty and blue.

When I saw four jackrabbits scampering down the hill toward us, I decided that everyone else was fixed on the preacher's words and hadn't noticed a thing. Suddenly a woman cut right in on the prayer and shouted, "Look at that cloud."

The minute I raised my eyes and saw the duster, I knew we were in trouble. I'd seen dozens of dust storms, but I'd never seen one that big and black. Dirt boiled off the ground and lifted into the sky as the main cloud rolled over the hill.

Everybody took off running for their wagons and cars. By the time we got to our truck, the wind had already hit. Dust was flying everywhere. As Daddy fired up the engine, I looked back at the cemetery. Two caretakers were trying to shovel some dirt into the grave so wolves and coyotes couldn't get at the body, but they had to give up. While one fellow closed the gate to keep cattle from wandering in, the other one snapped a picture of the storm. Then they hightailed it off with the rest of us.

Most of the folks headed back to Kenton, but Daddy started toward home. He said he was worried that we hadn't closed up the house as tight as we should have, and he didn't think he'd tied off our windmill. By the time we turned onto the highway, the main cloud was darker than a thunderhead and racing straight at us. "Is this the Judgment Day, C.J.?" Dalton asked as he and Belle squeezed close to me in the back of the pickup. I told him of course not, but it was hard for me to keep my voice from shaking. Ever since a big meteor was sighted over west Texas last spring, lots of people have been talking about the end of the world. Daddy and Mother both call that hogwash, but the preachers at camp meetings have been saying that these storms are the wrath of God, and that man is being smitten for his evil ways.

"This will all blow over shortly," I said, trying to ease the fears of the younguns. But I could tell they were not convinced. Dalton and Belle clamped onto my arms, and we sat stock-still, staring as the last blue light above Black Mesa was swallowed up.

Mother is calling for me to put out the lamp, so I'd better finish this tomorrow.

April 16

I'm sitting on the back porch watching the sun try to burn through the haze. Since everybody else is still sleeping, I'll tell the rest of that duster story.

It got darker and darker as the storm rushed toward us. The wind was quartering out of the north, and blasting the truck so hard that I was afraid we would tip right over. By the time we reached Carrizo Creek, the dust was so thick that Daddy couldn't see to drive. (He told me later that even with the headlights on he couldn't see as far as his radiator ornament.) By the time Daddy pulled over to the side of the road, blue sparks of static electricity were flashing above the hood, and Grandpa was coughing so loud that I could hear him over the sound of the sand rattling against the truck.

Our cab doesn't have side windows, so Daddy grabbed a blanket and had us all hunker down on the ground behind the pickup box. Though Grandpa was wheezing bad, he helped lift Belle down and hushed her crying. Mother told the younguns not to rub their eyes, but once you start scratching, it's terrible hard to stop.

I've heard folks talk about it being so dark that they couldn't see their hand in front of their face, and I figured they were stretching the truth, but when the full force of the storm hit, that's exactly how black it was.

About two hours later, the wind eased enough for us to crawl out from under the blanket. The dust had drifted flush with the running board on the lee side of the truck, and it was still getting deeper. Daddy said we'd better get going before the wind kicked up again. My eyes and nose were crusted with dirt, and my teeth felt so gritty that I would've paid cash money for a glass of water to rinse out my mouth. As we stood up, piles of dust trickled off our laps. Dalton and Belle were sniffling a little bit, but I was proud of how strong Lester and Olive were.

It was late by the time we limped back home. The visibility was so poor in spots that Daddy had me walk ahead of the truck and guide us so we wouldn't drive off into the prairie. When we finally got to the farm, we peeled back our dusty sheets and crawled into bed.

I hear Mother in the kitchen, so I'd better help her build a fire and fetch some water.

After Breakfast

When I woke up this morning, the only white spot on my pillow was where I'd laid my head. On my way to check the stock in the barn, the sky was so gray that it looked more like twilight than dawn. Tumbleweeds had caught in the barbed wire along our east field and trapped so much dirt that the whole fence row had disappeared under one long, gray drift. But the deepest dust pile of all was on the lee side of our barn. The cultivator was covered right up to its handles.

As I walked through the henhouse, I was amazed to see the head of a chicken sticking out of a dust pile. She was buried up to her neck. I thought for sure she was dead, but when I bent down and tapped her beak, she let out a weak cackle. After I dug her out, she shook the dust off, wobbled into the coop, and took her regular place on the roost. I was glad to see that the other chickens had had sense enough to take cover. We'd hate to lose any hens, 'cause eggs bring us a steady ten cents per dozen.

Cleaning up took a lot longer than it did after the last storm. Like Daddy feared, we had left a couple of windows cracked. So along with the usual layer of dust that covers everything inside the house after a big blow, little sand dunes had drifted all across the floor. If we had been home, we would have rolled up towels and laid them against the door and windowsills and checked the tape that we use to seal our windows. (The *Boise City News* office sells 500-foot rolls of gummed tape for 35 cents.) But no matter what we do, when the wind blows hard enough, there is no way to keep the dust out. Even with washcloths across our faces we end up breathing in lots of dust, and the air stays so hot and thick inside the house that it can snuff out a candle. For a day or two afterward our eyes are red and burning.

What makes the cleanup hardest is knowing that it's only a matter of time before the next dust storm rolls in. It would be easy to let things stay dirty, but Mother puts us all to work. We rough-sweep with brooms first. Then instead of mopping with water, which would turn the dust to mud, we polish the wood floors with a splash of kerosene. But there was so much dirt after this storm, I had to go after the biggest piles with a scoop shovel before we could begin our normal sweeping.

April 17

We finally have the house pretty well cleaned up. This morning when Mother saw me pull out my journal, she said, "You leave that book away until we get this house in order, or I'll send it back to Ruby."

Mother usually isn't one to complain, but she is getting tired of the dust. Not only does it dirty our clothes and our house, but it also blows so steady that it has worn the paint off every single building in the county. All we've got left around here are gray houses and gray fields bordered by gray fence posts.

Though the dirt was discouraging, the worst thing that happened during the storm was that our windmill got bent up. The machinery is still pumping, but it's making a grinding sound.

Grandpa is wheezing so bad that Mother called Doc Hall. We are afraid he might have dust pneumonia. By the time Doc got here Grandpa was coughing like his lungs were ready to bust. But Doc said it was a good sign that he was hacking up those big globs of dirt. Between coughs Doc had Grandpa swish out his mouth with warm water. Then he swabbed his nose with Vaseline, and he used an eyecup to rinse his eyes with boric acid.

Doc says we'll just have to make sure Grandpa rests easy and hope for the best.

April 18

I still can't believe it. I found a quarter eagle gold piece in the yard this morning before I walked to school! I'd just finished watering the cows, and I took a shortcut past the old half dugout house over yonder by the barn. (The dugout is the original homestead cabin that Grandpa and Grandma built on this property. It's partly dug into the ground and has a top half made out of wood that they hauled fifty miles by wagon all the way from Texhoma.) I was bumfuzzled to see a coin sparkling right on top of the bare ground until I remembered the Black Sunday duster. Finding things after a big storm is pretty common. The wind uncovers arrowheads and fossil bones and chunks of Indian pottery that you never dreamed were lying right under your feet. After a storm last month a farmer over by Guymon found a six-shooter, complete with a full cartridge belt and holster, only a few paces from his front stoop.

When I asked Grandpa whether he'd ever lost a gold coin by the front door of his old cabin, he grinned and said that in them days he was lucky to have a couple of Indian pennies in his pocket. He laughed so hard that he started coughing. That made me feel bad. But once he hacked up some black mud and got his breath back, he told me that it felt good to laugh for a change. Then he turned serious when he saw that the date on the coin was 1899. "Why, lookee there — 18 and 99 was your uncle Grant's birthday, C.J.," he said. He reminded me that Grant would have been thirty-six years old this very month, and he told me that I'd better save the coin as a good-luck piece. Just before he fell back asleep he grinned like a possum and said that ole rattler had probably bit me 'cause I was "treadin' too near his treasure."

School is dustier than ever. We've got big tall windows that don't seal very well. I wipe my desk off with my shirt sleeve a dozen times a day, but only a few minutes later there's enough dirt for me to draw in with my finger. A funny thing happened when we were playing baseball at recess. My buddy Jed Roberts tried to catch a pop fly, but the dust was so bad that he never saw the ball until it bopped him on the forehead. Jed is normally a sure-handed catcher, and the boys teased him something awful. By the time school was over his left eye had puffed up bad.

April 19

I stopped by Jed's house on the way home from school. We took our eighth-grade comprehensive examinations today. I felt sorry for Jed because he had to read those test questions with one eye swelled half shut. The Roberts have the biggest dust drift I have ever seen at their back door. It's as tall as the eaves of their house and stretches out eight or ten feet before it begins tapering down. Jed said it took him three hours of shoveling to clear a path to his door.

April 20

Folks have tried everything to stop the dust storms. A girl in my class, Ethel Snap, has an aunt up in Dodge City who's joined a prayer band that includes a passle of folks all across Kansas and Colorado. They pick a certain time and all pray for rain.

Lots of fellows have tried to invent rainmaking machines. (Me and Jed tried to think one up, but even with Jed's lively imagination, we couldn't make any headway.)

Folks are so desperate for rain that one Boise City man wrote a letter to President Roosevelt asking him to please come and visit us, because he heard that when the president toured the Dakotas it rained in every town he drove through. A crazy fellow named H.W. Young says that if the army had a practice war out here on the plains, the artillery fire would shake down some rain.

April 21

My lucky gold piece doesn't seem to be working.

Just when I thought things couldn't get any worse, our ceiling fell in. And when I say the ceiling fell in, I don't mean in a manner of speaking, I mean the doggone ceiling came right down on top of us.

It was breakfast time. Mother was cutting a piece of corn bread for Belle when I heard a tiny creaking above our heads. It sounded like a nail pulling out of a board, but before I could even tilt my head back to see where the sound was coming from, the whole ceiling came crashing down. Luckily we all managed to duck so our high-backed chairs kept the boards from hitting our heads.

Of course, that didn't save us from the dust. We were blinded by the mess. The dirt was fine like river silt or face powder and ankle-deep. Dalton and Belle started wailing so loud that we thought one or the other was hurt bad. But when Olive and I carried them outside and brushed them off, we found they was just plain scared.

April 22

Grandpa has been telling stories about his very first days in Cimarron County. He chuckles whenever he thinks back on how foolish he and Grandma felt when they arrived in Boise City and discovered that they had been swindled into buying worthless land. Grandma was all for heading back to Missouri, but Grandpa fell in love with the plains right from the start. He talked her into staying, and they filed a homestead claim on a quarter section southwest of town. They ranched and farmed, adding to their herd and seeding a few more acres every year.

In 1913 they picked up another quarter section, but a bad dry spell settled in. Though it pained Grandma and Grandpa to watch their crops fail, the hardest thing they had to face was the death of their oldest son, Grant, who burned up in a prairie fire when he was only fourteen years old. Grandma never talked about that day, but Grandpa just called it THE fire. He told me how the flames roared out of New Mexico and tore all the way to Texas before the fellows could plow firebreaks and stop it. Thousands of cattle died. Grandpa said you could see the bones lying in the sun for years afterward. Lots of ranchers went broke. Some fellows made money by hauling carcasses off to fertilizer plants, but Grandpa said he'd rather starve than be a "bone merchant."

Despite the hard times, Grandpa never lost his love for the land. But Grandma blamed the open range for taking her son. The older she got, the more she talked about the hills and the trees back in Ohio. The day before Grandma died I was sitting by her bedside. She was so weak that she hadn't talked in a long time, but all of a sudden she caught my hand and spoke clear. "This flat country makes me nervous, C.J.," she said. "I swear it pulls my eyes right out of my head."

Those were the last words I ever heard her say.

April 23

I finished the Zane Grey book that Daddy bought me. I had to grin when I found out the story was about a man who died in a desert dust storm. I like to read books that help me forget about the misery in these parts, but since Daddy can't read, he has to pick a book by the cover. He had no idea he was buying me a book filled with death and African dusters.

April 24

Grandpa is doing a whole lot better. With the help of his cane he can walk all the way from the bedroom to the kitchen.

April 25

I heard that a man down in Dalhart, Texas, has formed what he calls a "Last Man's Club." He took the name from an old Civil War unit. The only requirement to join the club is that you have to promise to stick out these hard times and not move away.

So many folks have left our township this spring that Grandpa joked that we Jacksons and the Roberts could be called the Last Families Club.

April 26

We listened to a brand new radio program over at Aunt Ruby's called *Fibber McGee and Molly.* I still prefer *Tarzan* and *The Lone Ranger,* but Olive and Ruby thought it was the funniest show ever.

More stories keep turning up about how bad our Black

Sunday dust storm was. It blew so hard that the wind gauge in Boise City broke. And according to the paper, dirt clouds blew as far east as Washington, D.C., and even blanketed a ship two hundred miles out to sea. Daddy hopes that will wake the politicians up to the fact that we've got problems. He knows President Roosevelt cares, but he doesn't trust those congressmen a lick. In fact, Franklin D. Roosevelt is about the only man other than Will Rogers that Daddy respects outside of Cimarron County. My mother admires Will Rogers, too, being that he is part Cherokee like her. She smiles whenever Mr. Rogers reminds folks that his ancestors didn't come over on the *Mayflower* — they were already here to meet the boat.

The strangest local news to come out of the storm is a picture that someone snapped of the biggest roller. They had it made into a postcard, and when people got to looking close at the shape of the cloud, they were amazed to see the face of old Reverend Guy, beard and all, outlined against the darkening sky!

Grandpa is walking around without his cane for the first time today, and he is in fine form with his teasing.

April 28

I was over visiting Jed Roberts this afternoon after church. Jed told me about a funeral that he went to on the same day we tried to bury William Guy. The Lucas family had a double ceremony for Grandma Lucas and her one-year-old great-granddaughter, Ruth Snell Shaw. The storm got so bad that those folks had to halt their procession and drive back to Boise City. When they got to the cemetery the next day to finish the service, they had to redig the grave, which had drifted full of dust.

For the last couple of weeks Jed and I have been working on a sail buggy. The thing I like about Jed is that he's always ready for an adventure. Mother calls him "a little feller with big ideas." Though most people have been complaining about how bad the wind is, Jed and I decided that instead of whining we should have some fun with it.

Jed's daddy let us borrow an old wagon. We took off the tongue, patched up the wagon bed, and tied a rope to each end of the front axle so we could steer. Then we rigged up some burlap sacks for a sail. At first we barely crept along, but as the sails filled out, we went faster and faster. Jed and I were whoopin' it up good and really flying when we passed Noblin Stringfellow driving toward Felt in his mule wagon. I know we could have sailed all the way to Beaver Creek or even Texas, but we realized it would be a lot harder coming back than it had been going out. So we pulled down our sail and coasted to a stop.

It was lucky we stopped when we did. The long, hot drag back to Jed's house was not fun. The worst part was meeting Noblin. He pulled up his mules and pointed his finger at us like he was aiming a buffalo gun. "You boys drag that fool contraption back to the junk pile where it belongs," he said, loud as a camp preacher ordering us to pray. "That should teach you not to wave so sassy at folks when you pass them by."

April 29

Though we are keeping a couple of milk cows, we sold our cattle to the Drought Relief Service men. We can't afford feed, and the last dust storm buried what was left of our pastureland. Even if we could feed the cattle, it wouldn't make sense with beef selling for next to nothing.

It hurts us all to watch the land die, choked and burnt, but I feel most sorry for Grandpa. He misses the old days and keeps talking about the fine grass of years gone by and the way things used to be. I can remember the party games that Grandpa used to lead back when I was a little boy. We would clear all the furniture out of the house to get ready. Then just before dark the neighbors would arrive in buggies, Model Ts, and saddle horses. Some even rode double on bareback mules. The singing and dancing went on long into the night. There were cakes and watermelons and cider and a whiskey jug that the fellows pulled on out back. Grandpa was a fine fiddler before his hands got crippled with arthritis, and he used to roll off a string of rhymes like nobody's business. "Skip to My Lou" was his favorite song, and he could work that one forever. He'd start off with regular lines like "Fly's in the buttermilk, Shoo, fly, shoo," but pretty soon he'd be putting everyone in stitches by singing "Pig in the parlor, bugs in the biscuits, cat in the cream jug, skeeter on the gatepost, chicken in the dough pan," pausing each time for the chorus to answer back. He must have knowed two hundred verses for that song. I wasn't supposed to stay up too late, but I always sneaked a peek to see what was going on.

Grandpa had to go inside when the Relief Service marksmen came to shoot our cattle. We only got paid a few dollars for each cow and three dollars for our calf. Daddy was hoping for more, but the men said they needed registration papers to pay a premium price. I hated to see them take that calf — she was a pretty little whiteface with big soft eyes — but they led them all away. We heard the shots a short while later. Daddy just lowered his eyes and shook his head. He'd tried to persuade the men not to let the meat go to waste. He even offered to take less money, but they said it was against the policy. Culling out stock was the only way to bring the prices in the meat markets back up. "Policy." Daddy repeated the word with a snarl like it was poison in his mouth. "What sort of a man would write a policy that feeds the buzzards, when there's younguns goin' to bed hungry?"

April 30

Grandpa has set aside a few dimes and promised to take us to a Hoot Gibson movie. Grandpa loves cowboy shows, and Hoot is his absolute favorite. When Mother tries to talk to him about what a fine singer Gene Autry is, Grandpa scoffs and says Autry is just a sissy boy who can't hold a candle to Hoot.

May 3

It snowed today! Just when we were thinking about planting our garden, we got a May Christmas. Dalton and Belle tried to build a snowman, but the snow picked up so much dirt as it was falling that they ended up making a big mud ball.

May 4

Despite the terrible dust storms that killed so many jackrabbits last month, thousands of those critters are still roaming the countryside. They are chewing up what little grass is left, and they will soon be getting into our gardens.

To kill some rabbits off we had a drive yesterday over at the Roberts' place. We started by lining up a bunch of folks on one end of the pasture. Then as we walked side by side, those on the outside pinched in, funneling the rabbits toward a round pen. In a short while we'd corralled three or four hundred rabbits. The men and boys stepped in with clubs and began knocking the rabbits over the head. The squealing was awful, but it's gotten to the point where it's either kill the rabbits or let them starve us.

In the middle of the rabbit drive poor Jed got another dose of bad luck when Myron Finch smacked his face as he was swinging his club back. It was only a glancing blow, but it caught Jed above the same eye that had just healed from his baseball accident. Daddy joked that we are going to have to start calling him Calamity Jed. Being a good-humored boy, Jed laughed right along with the rest of us.

When the clubbing was done, we divided up the rabbits. Daddy and I were careful to pick out young, healthy ones, because a disease has been going around among the mangier animals.

May 6

I read some more news in the paper about those crazy "Last Man" folks down in Dalhart. Last week they collected $300 and hired an explosive expert named Tex Thornton, who said he could bring rain by blowing up the clouds. Several thousand ranchers and farmers and newspaper reporters came out to watch, along with all the local politicians, of course. Thorton planned on sending up a bunch of hot-air balloons with timed explosives. However, the joke was on him when a dust storm blew in just as he was getting ready. It was too windy for him to use his balloons, but he was too stubborn to give up. So he planted sixty TNT charges in the ground and set them all off at once. Folks who were there said that not only did it not rain, but it also made that ole dust storm twice as mean.

Daddy says he wishes he could have been there to see the politicians run for cover.

May 9

Grandpa died yesterday. Even as I write this, I can't believe it's true. He seemed to be doing so well. The next thing we knew he was gone. Doc Hall said it can happen that way with dust pneumonia. People look to be all better, but once they get up and start moving, something jars loose inside them. Doc called it a "sudden relapse." Grandpa has been a part of my life as long as I can remember, and I can't begin to imagine what it will be like without him.

May 10

We had Grandpa's funeral today. Mother sang two hymns, and she held up a lot better than me or Daddy. It's been powerful hard on Daddy to bury two parents inside of seven months.

The minister spoke about the old days and how Grandpa was one of the original pioneers in the county, living as he had in the last days of the open range. He mentioned how Grandpa had ridden on several cattle drives with Mr. Charles Goodnight, a Texan who once ran a million-acre spread.

I talked with Mother this evening after all the neighbors had gone home, and she tried to help me sort through my sadness. She told me it's natural to miss Grandpa, but I should remember that he lived a good, long life. As true as that might be, I can't help feeling bad that he died like he did. It is sad that his doctor back in Ohio sent him to Oklahoma so he could escape that coal mine and breathe clean, dry air. Then he went and swallowed so much dust that it choked him to death.

May 15

For the first time ever my parents are talking about moving away. I was afraid that would happen. With the wheat blowed out and the pasture dead, our choices are getting fewer. Daddy says the money we got from the government cattle sale will buy enough gas to get us to California. He's heard there are lots of jobs out there. Mother doesn't seem so anxious. Neither do us kids, except for Olive, of course, who wants to see Hollywood.

Up until yesterday Daddy was talking about investing his cattle money in turkey chicks. Mother agreed that our played-out land might have enough left in it to raise a flock of turkeys. But on the day Daddy was going to the feed store to place his order for chicks, he found out that a pack of coyotes had got into Millard Fowler's turkeys. All that was left of Millard's 110 turkeys was 80 gizzards — the gizzard is about the only part other than the feet that those ornery critters won't eat — and a handful of strays. When Daddy heard that story, he set aside his turkey-raising plans real fast.

May 16

I can't get used to Grandpa being gone. He was the talker and the storyteller in our family, and it's way too quiet now.

Lester is taking it the hardest of all. Yet it's Dalton and Belle I feel sorriest for. The rest of us had lots of good times to share with Grandpa, and we have memories that dying can't ever take away. But they are both so little, that before long the only thing either of them will remember about Grandpa is his name.

That's the way it is for Jed Roberts. Both of his grandpas died before he was born, and he's always felt like there was something missing in his life. "At least you know where you come from," he's said to me more than once. Grandpa knew how Jed felt, and he always called Jed his "adopted grandson."

May 19

I slept so poorly last night that I almost dozed off in church today. We had a full moon, and even with the dust haze hanging in the air, the light was so bright that I couldn't settle down.

After church we had dinner at Aunt Ruby's. She was real proud of me when I told her I'd been writing regular in the journal she gave me. Aunt Ruby was a librarian before she married Uncle John, and she believes in the power of book learning. She said that lots of famous "men of letters" (a man of letters is not a mailman like it sounds but a fellow who does lots of reading and writing) kept journals. But when she told me the strange names of those fellows, like Aurelius, Pepys, Boswell, and Thoreau, I wasn't so sure if I wanted to join that club.

May 24

More folks are leaving our county every day. Olive cried this morning when she found out that one of her best friends, Tessie Boatwright, had moved away yesterday. Her daddy got so discouraged that he packed up the family and left without telling a soul. He didn't even bother to close the front door — just left it swinging in the wind.

May 25

Two bad things happened today.

One — jackrabbits got into our garden. The first shoots were just coming up, and they ate off every last sprig. I never killed a rabbit in all our rabbit drives, but I was so angry when I thought back to all the barrels of water we'd hauled to keep those plants alive, I would have clubbed one of those bunnies good.

Two — and this is the worst news of all — our windmill quit working. It wasn't even blowing hard when it happened. The blade just creaked to a stop. I figured Daddy, being the handy mechanic that he is, would get it pumping in no time. He fiddled with the machinery for a long time, then shook his head. "Them gears have finally gave out, C.J.," he said.

Without a windmill, we've got no water to drink or to use for washing, and no way to cool our milk and cream. That means we'll have to sell our last two cows.

May 26

After looking into the cost of parts, Daddy has decided that we can't afford to fix our windmill. For the last two days we've been hauling drinking water by the barrel from the Roberts' place. Even when I have Lester and Dalton sit on the barrel lids so they can't rattle loose, there is still a gray scum of dirt on top of the water by the time we get home.

Daddy's gotten more quiet than normal. He keeps shaking his head like he's been fooled by a trick that he can't quite figure out. We had a fine ranch just a few years ago, and now all that's left is a dead wheat field, one hog, and a few dusty chickens.

May 27

The strange weather continues. The sky darkened like we were going to have a thunderstorm, but instead of rain we got hail. I was down at the barn when it started, and it sounded like someone had dumped a box of rocks on the roof. The hailstones were as big as hen's eggs, and they broke all three windows on the west side of our house. The flying glass cut Dalton's foot, and during the worst of the storm, we had to hold quilts up to keep the hailstones from hitting the younguns.

May 28

We are moving out. Daddy boarded up our busted windows this morning and announced that we are heading west. He plans for us to find work out in California, save up some money, and then come back here after the weather turns normal again. This spring we've seen dozens of handbills advertising for workers in a place called the San Joaquin Valley. So that's where we will go. Everyone says there are thousands of jobs out there.

The thought of moving is scary, but being that Daddy promises it won't be permanent, I figure it might be fun picking oranges in the sunshine for a change. Lester agrees, and Olive is positively thrilled. Ever since Olive saw her first Shirley Temple movie, she has dreamed of moving to Hollywood and getting an actress job. Lately she's been practicing her soft-shoe and singing routine on the back porch. When Lester teases her, she just sings louder.

May 30

Daddy refuses to auction off our things like most of the farmers have. He knows there is no market for used farm equipment, and he's seen too many folks humiliated by having to take pennies for perfectly good implements.

He did sell our horses and chickens. We got $13 for the team (Daddy called that robbery) and 25 cents a piece for the laying hens. Jed will look after our milk cows, and Daddy is locking everything else up in the barn. That way when we come back we'll be set to start right in farming.

May 31

We are packed and ready to leave tomorrow morning. Daddy and I have rigged stake bed sides and a canvas top over the back of our truck to keep the younguns out of the sun. We have a two-wheeled trailer loaded with tools, clothes, kitchen things, bedsprings, mattresses, and bedding. To save room we've hung our washtubs and buckets on the sideboards. We rendered the hog and put the meat in a crock, and we've packed up flour, lard, cornmeal, beans, and potatoes so we can cook along the way.

After supper I borrowed Jed's horse and rode over to the cemetery to visit Grandpa's grave one last time. On the way I passed three abandoned houses. The saddest one of all was the Tucker farm. Mrs. Tucker had a fine plum thicket behind her house, but the dust has drifted so deep that the only thing left is a few dead branch tips poking out of the dirt. It was eerie watching their broken windmill spinning in the wind.

Later, as I stood in the darkness beside Grandpa's freshly mounded grave, I struggled with the truth of him being gone. When I close my eyes I can see him sitting in his same ole chair, rambling on like he always did about the old days. His voice would rise and fall as he spoke of the sweet times past: the spring floods on Beaver Creek, the summer rains that swept low across the prairie, and the grass that grew so rich and heavy that it rippled in the slightest wind.

I fingered the lucky gold piece in my pocket, and I whispered a little prayer to Grandpa. I told him to rest easy and that I would come back and visit him as soon as I could. I knew he would understand our taking a chance on a journey. When he left Ohio all those years ago, he was taking the same sort of gamble we are, and hoping there would be better times out west.

June 1, Near Wildorado, Texas

We are camped west of Amarillo, Texas. Though it's nearly time for bed, there is still plenty of light to write by.

My mind hasn't caught up to the fact that we are really on the road. As we pulled out of the yard this morning, I looked back on our ranch one last time. I thought of what Grandpa used to say about the Panhandle country. The drier things got, the more he talked about the green times of his youth. "Plant anything on this prairie, C.J.," he would say, mixing up the past with the present. "You just try her. She'll grow and grow."

I know that's true. I can remember running through fields of grain taller than my head when I was little. Daddy didn't even holler at me for knocking the wheat heads loose, because grain was growing as far as a man could see. Now the dust drifts get deeper every day, and the land lies as lifeless as Grandpa.

Our plan was to catch Route 66 in Amarillo and head for New Mexico. West Texas is even drier and hotter than home. Heat shimmers off the packed gravel and makes it hard to tell how far off things are. Pulling the trailer strains our truck and makes her smoke and rattle worse than normal. Our radiator boiled over three times today, and we're burning oil so bad that Daddy has to keep a gallon can on the floor up front. We swallowed so much road dirt that Mother joked that we might as well be back home fighting a duster.

We barely do twenty-five miles per hour, and our wooden-spoke wheels are wobbling bad. When the wheels dried out back home, it was easy to roll the car into Beaver Creek and let them swell up again. After a good soaking we'd pull the car out, and the wheels would be as tight as new.

Daddy hoped we could make it to the New Mexico border before nightfall, but we got a flat tire half way between Bushland and Wildorado. By the time we got the tire patched, it was so late that Daddy decided to set up camp. We pulled over beside a dry creek bed. There wasn't a twig or a cow chip in sight for firewood, so we ate a cold supper of corn bread and leftover beans. Dalton and Belle are asleep in the back of the pickup, but the rest of us have laid our blankets on the ground. I am proud of the younguns for not complaining one bit today. I've got a hunch there'll be plenty more cold meals and nights on the ground ahead.

June 2, Romero, New Mexico

I felt funny not going to church this morning, but I suspect it will be a while before we wear our Sunday-go-to-meeting clothes again. Though we were up before sunrise, it hadn't cooled more than a degree or two during the night. This must be one of the hottest places on earth. We ate the rest of our corn bread and beans for breakfast. Once the sun started beating down on our black truck, it went from hot to hotter. Mother said, "We'll be able to fry us some griddle cakes on that hood by lunchtime."

We keep a pail of water in the back and a washcloth to dab off Belle's face, but she's getting a bad heat rash on her neck. Olive tried to take Belle's mind off her misery by leading the younguns in some songs. She doesn't know as many verses of "Skip to My Lou" as Grandpa did, but she does a tolerable job with it.

Daddy and I switched off with the driving same as yesterday. When I take my turn Mother rides in the back. I can't believe the number of people who are heading west. We passed every sort of jalopy you can imagine. Lots of folks are pulling trailers like we are. A few are even trying to haul long-tongued farm wagons down the road. The craziest fellow of all was pushing a wooden wheelbarrow piled with stuff and painted with a sign that said CALIFORNIA OR BUST! I figure he is likely to bust.

When we go through towns, the local people give us some hard stares. Sometimes young folks point and laugh. Can't say as I blame them. With the angle iron and board sides that Daddy and I built out over our pickup box and the heaped trailer load we are dragging behind, I suspect I'd chuckle, too.

After we crossed the border into New Mexico, we ran into more of the same handbills that we saw in Texas:

1,000 PEA PICKERS WANTED
GOOD WAGES ALL SEASON

The posters are nailed to fence posts and telephone poles along the road. With all the cars driving toward California, I figure there must be hundreds of farms out there that need workers.

Most of New Mexico is dead and dry, but we ran across a pretty pool called the Blue Hole in Santa Rosa. It's an artesian spring that has rock walls and trees all around it.

We had more good luck outside of Santa Rosa when we met a nice Mexican man who helped us fix our wobbly wheels. We'd stopped to make lunch beside a river — I think it was called the Pecos — when this fellow came by in a wagon. As soon as Daddy mentioned that our wheels were shimmying, he offered to help. We drove our truck into a shallow pool and let the wheels soak good. Then he pulled it out with his mule team. Daddy offered him money, but he shook his head and said, "Just eat a fresh peach for me when you get to California."

One thing that is livening up our trip is all the Burma-

Shave signs alongside the road. As we drive along, the younguns stick their heads up and read them together. Even little Belle and Dalton pretend they can sound out the words, and they shout along with us. The best one we saw today was this:

WHEN CUTTING
WHISKERS YOU DON'T NEED
TO LEAVE ONE HALF
OF THEM FOR SEED
BURMA-SHAVE

We drove through some pretty mesa country south of Chaco Canyon. The rocks are so red that they look like someone painted them. As the roads get hillier, our truck has to work harder. Mother says if we don't blow an engine on this trip, the good Lord will have taken special care of us Jacksons.

June 3

Now that we have reached higher country, Daddy is cussing out Henry Ford. The rear-end gear in our truck makes it a "dog" on the hills. Mother and Olive have been working "Old Dan Tucker" today, and we've all been singing along. "Old Dan Tucker was down in town, Swinging those ladies round and round . . ."

The views are getting prettier by the mile. Once we climbed above the scrub brush, the pines grew taller, and the sky turned a brighter blue. The air has a clean, green smell, like we used to get back home as winter was shifting into spring.

Rows of mountain peaks loom to the west, but no matter how far we drive, they still seem a long way off. It's hard for me to imagine how rough it must have been for folks back in Grandpa's day who followed this same route by wagon on the Sante Fe Trail.

The air cooled off fast the minute the sun went down. After the furnace of west Texas, it was a major shock.

On our way through Sante Fe we drove past the Harvey House Hotel, which looked big enough to hold the whole population of Cimarron County. It's a long, white building with a row of white columns in front. Fellows in suits hold the doors for the rich folks. Daddy joked that he felt sorry for those rich people who were so weak that they couldn't even open a door for themselves.

We had worse trouble with the truck today. Just past Santa Fe our transmission band burned out. It's lucky that Daddy brought some extra parts along with his tools. I helped him open the transmission case, and he spliced a band out of hog hide. We lost a good part of the day, but it didn't cost us anything. Pulling the trailer is really beating up our poor Model T.

Along with our bad transmissions, we had another flat tire. Though it would have taken a good chunk of our money, Daddy is beginning to think that he should have bought new tubes and tires before we left home. Out here on the road, so many people are having trouble that mechanics are charging $3 for a used tire.

We stopped to gas up at a combination café and filling station called Joe's Place. The younguns were jumping-up-excited when they saw that Joe had a pet monkey sitting on his counter. The monkey wore a little red cap, and he really took a shine to Daddy. He climbed up Daddy's pant leg and hopped on his shoulders, chattering the whole time. He pulled Daddy's cap down over his eyes, pulled at his earlobe, and tickled his beard stubble. We laughed till our sides ached, and even Mother, who is not much given to chuckling, joined in.

June 4, East of Albuquerque, New Mexico

At breakfast Daddy discovered that the whole time we were laughing at that cute monkey yesterday, the joke was on us. Daddy realized it when he reached in his pocket. With a bumfuzzled look he said, "Lookee here," and turned his pocket inside out to show that it was empty. "That monkey went and pickpocketed me."

Mother laughed at the thought of her man being robbed by a monkey. "You suppose that little feller was a member of Pretty Boy Floyd's gang?" she teased Daddy, and the younguns all giggled.

Lucky for us, Mother keeps most of our money hidden in a pouch she sewed inside her dress. And lucky for me, that critter didn't get his hands on my gold piece.

We camped near a little town called Alameda not too far from a Pueblo Indian reservation. There's nothing left of the tube in our left rear tire. As a last resort Daddy tried an old trick this morning. He took the tube out. Then he sawed a slit in the side of the tire, and we tamped as much sand as we could into the hole. Finally he made a "bandage" out of canvas strips, and I helped him wrap it over the top of the tire.

I asked Daddy how far he figured we'd get, and all he said was, "No tellin'."

The cooler weather has helped Belle's heat rash, but it's too late for our pork. The heat turned it rancid, and we had to throw it all away. That leaves us with beans and corn mush to eat. Mother tried baking corn bread in her Dutch oven last night, but she decided it's easier to boil mush over an open fire.

June 5, Gallup, New Mexico

I miss having a table. It's hard to write sitting on the running board of our truck with my journal balanced on my knee, but Mother says I better get used to "camp-style authoring."

Our sand-filled tire is a real "thumper." From now on no one will be taking a nap while we're driving. We had to replace the "Band-Aid" on the tire a few times, but we went a whole day without getting a single flat!

It sure is clever of those Burma-Shave folks to put only one line on each sign and space them out like they do. Olive usually gets the jump on the reading, 'cause she's got the sharpest eyes. We're keeping track of our favorite signs, and the younguns have asked me to write them down in my journal. Daddy voted for this one as the best so far:

WHISKERS LONG
MADE SAMSON STRONG
BUT SAMSON'S GAL
SHE DONE
HIM WRONG
BURMA-SHAVE

Mother liked the Bible reference, but she objected to putting all the blame on Delilah. Daddy still wouldn't change his pick.

Along with the Burma-Shave signs there are dozens of Pepsi Cola billboards along Route 66. I get so thirsty that I would almost trade my gold piece for a cold bottle of Pepsi.

Past Albuquerque the highway ran due west through miles of eroded buttes and mesas. It's hard to imagine the power it took to wear away the earth from around those tall rock spires. I'll bet they had some real dusters out here a million years ago.

West of Laguna are some old lava flows, and at Thoreau we parked by a sign that marks the Continental Divide. They claim that if a raindrop were split in two up there, one half would flow to the Pacific and one half to the Atlantic. That's pretty silly talk, because it's so dry around Thoreau that if a raindrop ever did fall, it would only disappear in the dust.

When I took my turn in the back this afternoon, I kept the younguns entertained by retelling one of my favorite books, *Tarzan of the Apes.* Lester's eyes got big when I described the giant ape that tried to kill Tarzan.

June 6, Walnut Canyon, Arizona

Shortly after we crossed the Arizona state line this morning, we had to pass through an agricultural inspection station at Sanders. A runty-looking fellow in a uniform that was two sizes too big sneered at our license plate and said, "More Okies, eh?" Then he told us that we were coming from "an infested area," which meant we would have to turn over all our fruit and vegetables. Daddy said we didn't have nothing with us but a few pinto beans and a sack of cornmeal. I could tell that Mother didn't like him lying about the potatoes we'd stashed in the bottom of our crock, but we need to keep every scrap of food.

When the fellow found out that we didn't have any work lined up in Arizona, he said, "You best keep moving then. California's the place you Okies belong."

There was that *Okie* word again. As Daddy pulled away, I heard Mother tell the younguns that the fellow had no manners. "We are Oklahomans and proud of it," she finished in an extra-loud voice, "and don't let no man tell you otherwise."

I know Mother is right, but when low talk reduces us to Okies, it's hard for me not to feel small and ashamed.

But I forgot all about those fellows only a few miles later when we reached a place called the Painted Desert. It was so pretty that Daddy let me slow down to a crawl. Mother and the younguns oohed and aahed at the deep gullies and the tall mesas splashed with every shade of red from rusty orange and burnt gold to a bright blood color.

Only a few miles farther on we saw a meteor crater.

The hole was deep enough to drop a couple of houses in, and a man had built a tall stone house right beside it as an observation point. Just down the road in Holbrook, Arizona, we passed by a street show where a man was offering five dollars to anyone who dared wrassle a bear. I could tell Daddy was tempted to give it a try for all that money. But as soon as Mother saw the twinkle in his eye, she said, "Don't you even think about it, Lee Jackson."

Once we got back on the road we ran into a Burma-Shave sign that Dalton and Belle picked as their favorite:

EENY-MEENY
MINY-MO
SAVE YOUR SKIN
YOUR TIME
YOUR DOUGH
BURMA-SHAVE

We camped for the night near Walnut Canyon National Monument. Though we couldn't afford to drive into the park, Olive talked me into taking a hike so she could look at the pueblos and cliff houses. We didn't get a hundred yards from our truck when a big lizard popped out. He was a black, horny-headed thing, at least a foot long. Olive jumped back and screamed. I was scared, too, when he poked his tongue out, looking like he was ready to bite. By the time the lizard had ducked behind a rock, Olive was already hightailing it for the truck.

June 7, Walnut Canyon

I never thought I'd write in my journal this many days in a row, but something new is happening every day. We spent a second day here, after we had our worst mechanical trouble yet.

I didn't know what had happened at first. I was driving up a low hill. All of a sudden the truck died and started rolling backward. I hit the parking brake, but that never slowed her down a bit. The kids yelled, "Stop, C.J.!" as the trailer swung back and forth, but we kept going faster and faster.

"Ditch 'er!" Daddy finally yelled.

I cut the trailer hard toward a drainage ditch. Pots and pans clattered as the trailer jumped into the air. Belle screamed like she'd been bit by a bobcat, and the front left wheel lifted up. Luckily, just before we tipped over, the trailer hit the up slope, and we rattled to a stop.

"You done good," Daddy said, and he slapped my shoulder. But my knees were shaking so bad when I climbed out of the cab that I couldn't even talk.

It was a wonder we weren't all killed. When Daddy

pulled the axle, he found that the prongs on the oil seal had scored the shaft so deep that it broke clean off. "Good gosh almighty," he said, reading the part number, "Number 2511RE done all that damage." Then he gave Henry Ford another cussing for using such a poor design.

Daddy and I hitchhiked to Flagstaff and pulled an old axle off a wrecked car at a place called Jer's Junkyard. Jer said he had never seen a fellow spin a wrench as fast as Daddy.

June 8, Kingman, Arizona

West of Flagstaff we passed through a pretty pine grove. Then the land gradually turned hard and dry. We made good time, traveling through Williams, Ash Fork, Seligman, and Peach Springs (not a peach tree in sight). I'm tired of writing down the names of all the towns, but the younguns insist that I record every one.

We saw another Burma-Shave sign that tickled Belle and Dalton. Olive complained they had no right to pick a second one, but I told her that because there were two of them, they got two votes:

BENEATH THIS STONE
LIES ELMER GUSH

TICKLED TO DEATH
BY HIS SHAVING BRUSH
BURMA-SHAVE

When we drove past the turn for the Grand Canyon without even slowing down, Olive nearly cried, but Daddy said he'd seen plenty of big holes in his day and wasn't about to detour to see another.

The camp here in Kingman is so dry that they charge ten cents a bucket for water — as much as a gallon of gas. Everyone says the Black Mountains, which lie just ahead, will be worse than anything we've yet seen.

Dalton and Lester had fun playing Run Sheep Run and Drop the Handkerchief with some other boys in camp, but they both admit they are "sung out" and tired of the road. Before Belle went to sleep she asked me if California is as far away as China.

June 9, Sitgreaves Pass, Arizona

Sunday was no day of rest for us. We camped for the night next to Edgerton's gas station. Mr. Edgerton warned us about a desert between here and Oatman, which he called "the biggest car cemetery in the United States." Mr. Edgerton's store is filled with things he has taken in trade for gas from people who have run out of money. He's got everything from guns and spare tires to watches and wedding rings. He said one lady even tried to swap her pet canary for a gallon of gas.

Since our hog-hide replacement for the transmission band has been slipping bad, Daddy put in a new one tonight. He figures that's the only way we'll make the steep grade ahead. On the shoulder of Route 66 near Edgerton's station there is a sign next to a dead-looking cholla cactus that says,

CARRY WATER
OR
THIS IS WHAT YOU'LL LOOK LIKE

June 10, South of Oatman, Arizona

We headed toward the Black Mountains two hours before dawn. The foothills weren't bad, but once we hit the main slope, our truck ground to a halt. We unhooked the trailer and stood for a while. One look at the household goods scattered along the ditch made it clear what he had to do, but Mother didn't want to face it. Though it was hot as Hades, Daddy let her talk it all out.

Finally Mother nodded. The trailer was the first thing

to go. Daddy and I eased it onto the road shoulder. Then we pried off the best boards and used them to reinforce the stake bed sides on the truck. Next, using the old nails for hooks, we hung up the pails and basins. Mother never blinked as we tossed away two crocks, three mattresses, and her bedspring. But when we picked up her cedar hope chest, she teared up bad.

Free of the trailer, Daddy revved up the truck and gave the hill another try, but she still gave out. "No-good, gutless engine," Daddy said, kicking at a tire.

Our only choice was to have everyone walk up the mountain. We filled two washtubs. Mother and Olive took one, and I was about to pick up the other when Daddy shook his head and said, "You're lots lighter than me, C.J. I think you'd best drive the rig." Mother said no at first, but Daddy finally convinced her that I'd have the best chance of making it.

It was tricky driving because our reverse gear was the only one with any power to climb. That meant I had to drive up the mountain backward. As I turned hard left and then right, following the hairpin turns, the muscles in my neck burned as bad as my leg did on the day I was snake bit. Yet I kept a death grip on the steering wheel, knowing one slip would be my last.

When I finally made it to the top, my hands were

cramped and the back of my shirt was soaked clear through. A big canvas-topped truck was pulled over in the other lane. The driver, who was letting his engine cool, congratulated me on my driving. "I wouldn't care to pilot no jalopy backward up that mountain," he said, looking down the slope. He told me he was hauling a load of cantaloupes from the Imperial Valley to Chicago. He was such a nice fellow that he gave me two cantaloupes free. "That'll give you your first taste of California, son," he said.

I thanked him and scooted back down the hill to help with the load. Later, when the younguns saw that fruit, their eyes just about popped out of their heads. "Melons," Dalton squealed, and Daddy got out his jackknife and split them open. As that sweet juice ran down my chin, I almost forgot that we were standing in the middle of nowhere with a good portion of what we owned in this life lost in a ditch down yonder.

Toward Evening

We reached the California border. Nothing ever looked so fine as when we came out of those burnt hills above Topock and saw the Colorado River. Daddy drove right up to the bank and parked. "Lordy be," he said, "would you look at all that water." Then he kicked off his boots and waded into the river with his overalls still on. As Daddy let out a big sigh and sat on the bottom, we all ran whooping down the bank and jumped in.

While the younguns splashed near shore, I walked to the edge of a reed bed and sat down. The water was bathtub-warm. I rested in the river a long time, letting a quiet peace wash over me and not even hearing the kids carrying on by the shore or the cars rumbling down Route 66.

That calm feeling was turned upside down only a short while later. My britches were still itching from my swim when we ran into some nasty guards at the California border. Without so much as a Howdy or a How you all doing? They spat out a million questions: Where you headed? How much money do you got? What's your business in our state?, never giving Daddy time to answer.

Then they rifled through the back of our truck and took our last potatoes, claiming that our little pile of spuds presented a danger to every farm in California. As we were pulling away, I heard one of the fellows mumble, "Those damned Okies are like flies around an outhouse. You swat one and a dozen more show up."

There was that *Okie* word again. The way this man said it hurt worse than that puff-chested inspector back on the Arizona border. This fellow made me feel like Okie meant dirt or something even worse.

June 11, Newberry Springs, California

I still get steamed when I think of those guards. Will Rogers once said, "Everybody is ignorant. Only on different subjects." Well, I think those haughty-mouthed fellows are ignorant on every subject.

Though we could have made it farther yesterday, we stopped at a place called Needles to rest up for tomorrow. I figured that once we hit California, it would be an easy drive to Bakersfield, the town where all the jobs are supposed to be. But across the Colorado River lies the deadliest stretch of driving we've yet faced — the Mojave Desert. Since daytime temperatures hit 120 degrees, most folks don't risk driving it until after dark.

While we were waiting for the sun to go down, Mother told me a story about the time her daddy arrested a half-dozen cattle thieves. I never met my Grandpa Cole, and hearing stories helps me imagine what he was like. He was the sheriff on a Cherokee reservation in western Oklahoma, and he never took sassing off nobody. Along with a big Colt pistol, he carried his "persuader," a sawed off ten-gauge double-barrel shotgun loaded with horseshoe nails, across his saddle horn.

We set out well after dark. Our plan was to take it slow and keep a close eye on the temperature gauge. At first Olive was leading the younguns in singing "Weevilly

Wheat," but after a few choruses they got tired and fell asleep.

It was so peaceful with the white stars burning above that it was easy to forget what a dangerous place the desert can be. Knowing rattlers mainly hunt at night, I was worried that we would have a breakdown and end up parking next to a den full of them. Except for the rough clattering of our engine and the occasional roar of a big Hudson or Packard flying by, it felt like we were all alone, sailing in a ship across an empty, black ocean.

The Burma-Shave signs continued even in the desert. They looked out of place, flashing in the headlights. But shortly after the younguns fell asleep I saw a funny one that I memorized so I could tell it to them when they woke up.

We got a scare when our engine sputtered and quit in the middle of the desert. I'd already decided that if we had to camp out here, I would rather sleep standing up than turn myself into rattler bait. Luckily Daddy had a hunch what was wrong. We lifted up the hood, and I held a lantern while he worked. When a horny toad hopped out from under the car, I jerked back so fast that I nearly started Daddy's beard on fire. Daddy said he could understand my being skittish about snakes, but if I didn't quit bouncing the light around he'd never get the job done.

Once I steadied down, it only took him a few minutes to pull the brass screen out of the sediment bulb and clean the dirt off. Before we started off I told everyone about those Burma-Shave lines I'd seen, and they thought they were so funny that they made me dig out my journal and write them down.

THE BEARDED LADY
TRIED A JAR
SHE'S NOW
A FAMOUS
MOVIE STAR
BURMA-SHAVE

We stopped twice to add water to the radiator (the highway department leaves barrels of water beside the road for drivers to use), and we had to top off our oil once, too. Just after midnight we pulled over and helped some folks who were stalled in an old Ford. It only took Daddy a minute to tighten their fan belt-adjusting screw. They tried to give him a quarter, but Daddy said it wouldn't be right for him to profit from another man's trouble.

We are now camped with some other folks at a pretty place called Newberry Springs. There's a patch of tall cottonwoods, a spring, and a shady patch of mesquite trees covered with wild grapevines. Just before dark someone pulled out a guitar, and a lonesome folk song was soon drifting out over the campfires:

Takes a worried man to sing a worried song
I might be worried now
But I won't be worried long.

Olive and Mother walked over and joined in the singing. A few minutes later a fellow pulled out a harmonica, and another man fetched a fiddle from his car.

As I listened to the song build into a chorus and watched the sky go pale, I had a strong feeling that we'd made the right choice in coming west. For if the rest of California turns out to be half as sweet as this little grove, it will be a fine place indeed.

June 12, Tehachapi

We started well before dawn again. In Barstow we ran into another ornery batch of inspectors. Daddy told them we didn't have any fruit or vegetables, but they made us wake up the younguns and unload every single thing.

Then they shined their flashlights inside the pickup box. Daddy was mad they'd woke the children, and it made him madder that they didn't trust us. He told one of the fellows that where he came from, a man's word was his bond. Little Belle was crying softly.

A different fellow stepped toward Daddy and said, "We don't take no lip from Okies."

I saw Daddy clench his fist, but Mother touched his shoulder quick. "Just let these men finish, Lee," she said. "Then I'm sure we can be on our way."

"You got a smart missus, Lee," one of the guards drawled, intentionally shining his flashlight straight into Daddy's face. "That's real good advice, 'cause we got lots of room in our jail for vagrant trash."

Daddy never said a thing, but I could tell he was smoldering mad. At slaughtering time I've seen him knock a steer dead with one blow from a horseshoe hammer, and he had that same steely look in his eyes. But he never said a word. As we got ready to pull out I wanted to tell that guard how lucky he was that Daddy hadn't taught him a lesson, but I held my tongue.

Outside of Barstow we left Route 66 and followed a state road through another stretch of flat, dry country. Then we climbed up a low range of mountains called the Tehachapi. At first I was afraid we might run into tight switchback turns like we had in Kingman, but the grade stayed gentle.

The sun was fully up behind us as we crept over the last rise. I'd just taken my turn at the wheel, and Mother was riding in back with the younguns. With the sun lighting up the black lava rocks on either side of the road, it looked like the dry land was never going to end. Then I caught a glimpse of a long valley. There was a dried-out lake bed ahead to the right, but beyond it, the desert brown blended into a bright green.

"Would you look at that?" Daddy whispered. I pulled over to the side of the road.

"What's wrong?" Mother called from the back, sounding like she was worried that we'd broke down.

"Come and have a lookee, Cleo," Daddy called. We got out of the cab, and Mother climbed down to join us. Olive and Lester poked their sleepy heads out, too. We stared wide-eyed at the distant green. I hadn't ever seen anything that bright and alive.

Later

The San Joaquin Valley is a deep green checkerboard of orchards and grapevines and vegetable fields that lies between the coastal mountains and an inland range. Along with the field crops there are ranches, almond groves, hay meadows, and cotton farms. Instead of planting a mess of things side by side like you do on a normal truck farm, these Californians set aside one big plot for tomatoes, another one for cucumbers, and so on. We even saw a field that was planted with nothing but eggplants. Daddy kept saying that if only we could get us a little chunk of land, we could raise enough in one summer to feed ourselves for ten years.

As our truck chugged past the farms, the younguns were so excited that they started singing in the back. Though Olive might get off pitch at times, her lungs sure are strong. Before long Mother and I joined in, too. Daddy even whistled along with us.

The one thing that seemed odd to me was the lack of people and farm buildings. In all the fields that we passed, I only saw a man or two driving along a fence line in a pickup truck.

Then just before we got to the city limits of Bakersfield we got our first bad news. There was a big sign:

NO JOBS HERE!

IF YOU ARE LOOKING FOR YOUR WORK — KEEP OUT!

TEN MEN FOR EVERY JOB!

I got a sick feeling when I saw those words. Daddy and Mother tried to hide their frowns, but Dalton, who was sitting on Mother's lap at the time, read her face and asked what was wrong. She said the only thing a mother could: "Don't you worry none."

On our way into Bakersfield we saw one more sign, and we got plenty of unfriendly stares. When we stopped at a gas station, my sick feeling was multiplied by a hundred times. I opened the door of the rest room, and I couldn't believe my eyes. After all the miles we'd put behind us, how could it come to this? Dalton, who was right beside me, saw it, too. "What's them words say, C.J.?" he asked, pointing at the scrawled letters above the toilet: OKIE DRINKING FOUNTAIN. I coughed back my anger and told him it just said to make sure to wash your hands.

Only a few days ago I didn't have any idea what an Okie was, but now I know. *Okie* means a man who is broke and down on his luck and ain't wanted nowhere. These folks think we're something less than human, and they're afraid to death that they might have to share a tiny part of their fine green country with us.

June 13, Hooverville

Yesterday we ended up parking in the only place we are allowed in Bakersfield. It's called Hooverville as a joke because it's filled with people who blame President Hoover for causing the Depression and all the unemployment.

When we pulled into the camp, the fire pits were still smoldering from breakfast. Daddy shut off the engine and got out to see where we could park, but Mother just sat in the truck and stared. It took Olive saying she would die before she would stay in a place like this to jolt Mother awake to hush her.

The camp next to Hooverville is called Hollywood. That's another joke, because both of them are an awful mess. About thirty or forty makeshift shacks are clustered together beside the river. The shacks are built out of stuff scrounged from the local dump: cardboard boxes, scrap lumber, stained pieces of linoleum, packing crates, rusty sheets of corrugated tin, and mildewed carpet. A few of the shacks have coffee-can chimneys sticking out of their roofs. Every place has a beat-up old jalopy parked beside it. Some of the vehicles look to be in running condition. Others have flat tires, or they're blocked up on chunks of wood so fellows can work on them. Oil pans, seized-up bearings, scorched pistons, and greasy wrenches are scattered across the ground.

Along with the shacks are a mix of gray tents, lean-tos, and brush huts made from grass and driftwood that people dragged up from the river. Faded dresses and overalls hang from tree branches and sagging clotheslines. I thought someone would come up and greet us, but they all turned and went back to their work.

So much for our welcome to sunny California.

June 15

Lester asked me why I didn't write in my journal yesterday. The reason, which I didn't tell him, is that I don't have the stomach to write down anything more about the awful ugliness of this camp. Back when we were on the road, even if it got hot and boring, I always knew there would be a mountain, or a mesa, or a pretty patch of pines coming up. Now we're stuck on a riverbank with nothing but smoke and dirt and a stench that won't go away. I think Mother knows how I feel, because she told Lester to leave me be.

Lester said he didn't mean to bother me but would I please read him some of those Burma-Shave jingles. When I leafed through my journal and started reading one, Belle and Dalton came and listened, too. Once I read the first line, they all joined in and recited the rest of the poem on their own. They remembered the whole thing and paused after each line as if we were still back on the road, waiting for the next sign to pop up:

BENEATH THIS STONE
LIES ELMER GUSH
TICKLED TO DEATH
BY HIS SHAVING BRUSH
BURMA-SHAVE

June 16

A lady finally came over and visited with Mother this morning. It might have helped that Daddy showed her husband how to fix his distributor. Word has already got around camp that Daddy is the man to talk to if you need help with your automobile.

The lady is from Liberal, Kansas, and she apologized for taking so long to introduce herself, but she said you can't be none too careful about who you talk to these days. I wish Mother would have asked her what she meant by that.

After lunch we drove over to a grocery story and bought a few potatoes, some cornmeal, lard, and bologna. The prices were real high. Though Mother and Daddy never said anything about our money, their faces told me we were down to our last pennies. I thought about offering them my gold coin, but I figured I'd better hold on to it for now. We got lots of mean looks as we drove down the street, and I saw two OKIE GO HOME signs.

As we were climbing back into the truck with our grocery sack, a little boy no bigger than Lester shouted, "Okie, Okie, dirty stinkin' Okie." Then he ducked around the corner laughing.

Daddy, who looked like he wanted to run after that boy, told the younguns, "Don't you all pay that hogwash no mind." But Dalton and Belle were already crying, and it took Mother and Olive a good long while to settle them down.

June 17

I can't believe the flies around this camp. Since there are no outhouses, people just use the bushes. With the temperature topping ninety every day, the smell is getting worse all the time. The only clean water is a far piece up the road. Lester and I take turns carrying the buckets, but the handles cut into our hands pretty bad. Some of the ladies use river water for washing dishes, but Mother won't hear of it.

We've been meeting more folks. There are people here from all over the Midwest and the South. Lots of them are tenant farmers and sharecroppers who went bust, but there are also a few landed families like ourselves that had to pull up stakes and move because of the drought or the Depression.

A fellow camper named Clem Arbogast stopped and visited by our fire this evening. Daddy asked him why there were so many people out here and so few jobs. "What about all them handbills?" Daddy asked, referring to the papers we'd seen along Route 66.

"We've all seen them," Clem laughed. Then he walked over to his car and brought back a wrinkled sheet of paper. "There was hundreds of ones like this back in Missouri," he said.

My eyes popped out. 1,000 PEA PICKERS WANTED, the writing said. It was the same handbill we'd seen all across Texas and New Mexico.

June 18

This morning Daddy and I went scouting for job prospects. We drove past miles of farms and orchards, but no one looked to be hiring. We even saw one sign that said

NO JOBS HERE, and another that read KEEP ON MOVING. Daddy kept saying that if only we could talk a fellow into letting us work an acre or two of this rich ground we would be sitting pretty. Big patches are lying fallow, which is a terrible waste with so many folks going hungry.

When we turned down a side road and saw a passel of melon pickers in a field, Daddy decided to ask if they needed more help. Daddy walked up to one of the managers. He was a short, flabby-jowled man, holding a clipboard and wearing a cowboy hat that made his head look small. He laughed when he saw how tall Daddy was. He shouted at one of his buddies and told him to look at the scarecrow that had just blown in.

When Daddy asked him if there might be a chance for him and me to apply for work, the man laughed louder. "You Okies and Texicans are too tall for stoop labor," he said, talking like he was the smartest fellow in the whole world and had written a book on the subject. "We want the short ones — the Mexies and the Japs. They squat real good."

I was afraid Daddy would blow up at him, but he just turned and shuffled back toward our truck. "Well, I'll be," was all he said, and he repeated it twice more as we drove up the road. It was like Daddy had been hit with so many insults since we got to California, he'd gone numb.

After we got back to camp I walked over to that grocery store on my own. I figured our luck couldn't turn any worse whether I had my gold piece or not, and it wasn't right for me to have that coin going to waste in my pocket while Dalton and Belle were turning over in their sleep at night and crying with empty stomachs. I figured to buy some bacon and beans and bread, and maybe even a few sticks of candy for the younguns.

As I walked through the door, a fat, aproned fellow behind the cash register sneered at me, and said to the man next to him, "What sort of trash you figure that is, Ralph, Arkie or Okie?" If the younguns wouldn't have been so hungry, I'd have turned around and walked right out of there. Instead I walked back to the butcher's counter and asked for two pounds of bacon. The butcher looked at me and said, "You got any cash money, boy? We don't do no barterin' in this here store." I nodded and held out my coin. He glanced at my palm and laughed, "We don't take no counterfeit coins neither." Then he slapped at my hand and knocked my quarter eagle gold piece right to the floor.

I stared as the coin rolled to a stop on the worn wooden floor. At first I felt a powerful urge to scream at him and tell him that my coin was real and that he'd better take it or else. Then my mind went calm. No, the slap of that butcher's bloody hand must be a sign telling me this is not a place for a man to be wasting his time.

June 19

Earlier this evening Mother was frying up the last of our bologna when she noticed Clem Arbogast's two boys standing a ways off and staring at her. We didn't have near enough for ourselves, but one look at the sunken eyes of those little fellers was more than Mother could stand. After she handed us our plates, she called Clem's boys over and offered them each a slice. Even if it meant she and Daddy were only left with a bit of bread and the pan drippings, Mother wasn't about to let those younguns go hungry.

The last two nights a boy has been playing a guitar and singing. He keeps repeating a song that sure doesn't improve the dreary mood of this place:

Lord, I'm going down the road feeling bad.
Lord, I'm going down the road feeling bad.
Lord, I'm going down the road feeling bad.
And I ain't goin' to be treated this-a-way.

The other verses talk about eating only "corn bread and beans" and "goin' where the climate fits his clothes" and how all his things added together will fit inside a matchbox.

He's not a bad singer, but I sure wish he would find a happier song. I asked Olive if she'd go over and join in with something livelier, but she said she don't feel like singing right now. I've never heard her say that before.

June 20

Daddy and I finally got a job. It's only temporary, but it's better than nothing. Just after daybreak a foreman stopped by the camp in a flatbed truck. He said he was looking to hire some men to pitch hay. Without bothering to ask how much it paid, a half dozen of us climbed onto the truck and he drove off. Lester wanted to go bad, but the man told him he was too scrawny.

When the truck turned into a driveway, I looked at the sign and thought it was a joke. HOOVER RANCH, it said. I figured the owner of the place had put up that sign to make fun of President Hoover, like the fellows who named our ditch bank camp. But a man who'd worked the ranch before told me and Daddy that the place is honest to God owned by relatives of President Hoover!

The Hoovers don't pay much — only 25 cents an hour — but it will put gas in our truck and keep us from starving. Whatever the wages, it feels good to get away from camp and drink in the smell of sunshine and fresh-cut hay. I can see why the crops grow so thick around here. Not only do they have good soil and hot weather, but most of the farms are also ditched for irrigation. As long as the rivers keep running, they've got no fear of a dust bowl out here.

The best part of working ten straight hours is that I will sleep real solid. I'm so worn out tonight that I don't care if I lay my blanket out in Hooverville or Hollywood — and by Hollywood I mean the real thing that Olive talks about all the time, not that dirty camp next door to us.

June 22

In one more day we should have the last of the hay crop put up for the Hoovers. I've been watching the stubble fields, and I can see that the grass grows more in a week out here than it does in a month back home. I don't doubt that they can get a half-dozen cuttings off their fields in a single season.

As green and as rich as this country is, I've had a powerful feeling of being closed in lately. I miss looking out and seeing nothing but the plains stretching open and free between me and the sky. Here everything has a tight, blocked-up feel to it, like they are trying to make the land into something that it isn't meant to be.

June 23

Mother and Olive and a few of the ladies in camp got together this morning and sang hymns. I thought of Grandma and how she loved group singing. She used to live for the Sundays when our preacher kept his service going long into the afternoon. At least once a month we'd have what Grandma called "preachin' all day, and dinner on the ground." The dinner always turned into a contest among the ladies to see who could bring the finest dish.

June 24

A bindle stiff walked into camp this evening just before dark. He carried a blanket roll over his shoulder like single fellows often do. After he took a good look around the camp, he strolled back to our fire.

Daddy said howdy and offered him a cup of coffee. He thanked Daddy kindly and tipped his cap to Mother as he took a seat on his bundle. He introduced himself as

Bob and said he'd been on the road for a long time. After a few sips of coffee, Bob settled back and sighed. "I could tell right off you were regular folks," he said, "but a fellow's got to be careful, you know."

Here was more talk about being careful. Before I missed my chance, I asked him right out what he meant.

At first he looked surprised. Then he said, "You must be new to the valley." When we all nodded, he explained that there had been lots of strikes against the big farms in the last couple of years. The growers had hired special detectives to spy around the labor camps and report on any union organizing. They also kept wages down by making sure there was an oversupply of workers. "I'll bet you've seen some handbills on your way out here," he said.

Daddy nodded, and Bob explained that it was part of the plan. With all the big machinery it only took a dozen men to manage a big orchard or a farm for most of the year, but when the crops came in, they might need a thousand or more workers all at once. "If five men show up for every job," Bob said, "instead of paying a nickel for a box of peaches, they'll drop her down as far as they can."

"They pay a nickel for picking a whole box?" Daddy asked.

"That's right," he nodded.

June 25

Daddy visited again with Bob over breakfast. We only had fried mush, but Bob didn't seem to mind. Daddy told Bob he still couldn't believe that spies would bother to come around a place like this, but Bob insisted it was a fact. According to him, the big growers were so set on stopping farmworkers' unions that they had formed a group called the Associated Farmers.

Daddy looked at Bob nervouslike and said, "You ain't one of them Wobblies are you?" Daddy views the Wobblies or IWW — that's Industrial Workers of the World — men as anti-American rabble-rousers.

Bob shook his head and said he'd been with a group called the Cannery and Agricultural Workers Industrial Union, which had just gone bust. He told about strikes in Tulare and Pixley and Arvin where farmers, along with the help of the police and hired thugs, had clubbed and teargassed the strikers. Then they locked them up in special stockades right along with the lawyers who had volunteered to help them.

When Daddy shook his head like he couldn't believe it, Bob said, "It's all true." He said another trick they used against a man who was pushing for higher wages was to accuse him of being a communist. Since the farmers shared their files with the police and the FBI, it was only a matter of time before that fellow was locked up, too.

Daddy insisted that folks must get fair trials in California, but Bob said, "Money can buy anything, including the law." Then he ticked off a list of other strikes that had been broken in San Jose and Santa Rosa, describing crosses burning on hillsides, vigilante farmers swinging pickax handles, college and high school football players wielding clubs and guns, and innocent folks being tarred and feathered. He finished by saying, "The Tagus Ranch even had a machine gun mounted on their truck."

Daddy looked doubtful, but Bob's talk made me nervous. We'd planned on driving out here and picking enough oranges to pay for the taxes on our farm, but we hadn't touched an orange yet, and things were looking more complicated by the minute.

Even after Bob had picked up his bundle and said good-bye, Daddy was still shaking his head. But only a few minutes later, any doubts he had about Bob's stories were shot clear away. I'd just grabbed a bucket to fetch water when we heard a siren. A minute later, two police cars pulled into camp and slammed on their brakes. Most of the folks ducked into their shacks or lit out for the brush, but we just stood there openmouthed.

Four cops piled out. They all carried police clubs, except for one who was holding a chromed pistol. They swaggered through camp like they were the kings of the world. The one with the pistol was the first to talk. He aimed his gun at Daddy's chest and said, "You all seen any agitators or commie pinkos around here?"

June 26

I sure am glad Daddy didn't go after that cop yesterday. By his face I could tell he was itching to teach him a lesson, but he held himself back. For the rest of the day Daddy kept shaking his head. Now that he'd seen how those cops treated regular folks like us, he reckoned that Bob had told us the truth. Since Daddy has always taught me that I needn't fear the law if I lead an honest and upright life, it was hard for him to admit that might not be the case here in California.

I'm learning to tell how long a person has been in the Hooverville camp by looking at them. Folks like us who have just arrived have a confused look on their faces, as if they are wondering whether they took a wrong turn and ended up somewhere other than California.

The folks who've been here a little longer have angry looks. It's not the quick, hot anger you get from being smacked or hollered at. It's a steady, burning anger that is set so firm on their faces it tells the world: somebody better do something real quick or I'm going to explode.

The folks who've been here the longest are the easiest to pick out. They're the ones who have given up altogether. Their eyes are dull and vacant. Their shoulders are slumped, and they walk with a slow, dragging shuffle. They are so numb from all the bad things that have happened to them, you could stick a .45 revolver in their face and they wouldn't even blink.

June 27

Daddy still hasn't given up looking for work. Though the folks around camp tell him there is no use in burning up gas driving around, he and Lester and I head up the highway and look every day.

Tonight after supper two young men from Oklahoma stopped by our camp with a guitar and harmonica. They played some old folk tunes, and Mother and Olive joined in. The fellow with the guitar sang a song that I'd never heard before:

Rather drink muddy water
And sleep in a hollow log
Than to be in California
Treated like a dirty dog.

June 28

I'm hurting today, but it's a good hurt. We got our first picking job this morning. Though my arms and legs are sore, it sure feels better working than sitting around this dreary camp.

A foreman came by at the crack of dawn and asked if anyone wanted to pick peaches. By the time the late sleepers had thrown off their blankets, we'd taken off after him.

Mother and Olive stayed behind to watch the younguns, but Lester came along. The caravan of cars drove a lot faster than our ole Model T was used to, but Daddy pushed our engine hard because he was afraid we would be left behind.

When we turned down the road to the orchard, we all stared. I have never seen so many peaches. There was one row after another, and every tree was sagging from the weight of ripe fruit. I could see why Daddy and I hadn't found work driving the main highways — lots of the big farms are off on little side roads.

They call picking peaches "ladder work," meaning you mainly work high. The first time I climbed into the tree, I found it was a lot trickier than scooting up a ladder that's leaning against something solid like eaves or a barn wall. The ladder tilts if you lean too far to one side, and when the breeze blows, you sway right along with the crown of the tree. To pick fast you have to balance on a rung and leave both hands free to fill your sack. I was careful not to snap off any branches, because the foreman said we'd be down the road if we busted up his trees.

I expected it to be cool working in a shady orchard, but after scrambling up and down that ladder and lugging a couple of loads of peaches to the truck, I was sweating bad. The sweet smell of the peaches, which was like perfume at first, almost made me sick. My dizzy feeling might have come from being so hungry and wanting in the worst way to chaw down a fresh peach.

As I unloaded my sack, a man kept a tally sheet to record how many boxes I picked. The first time, I dumped the fruit a little too quick, and he yelled, "Bruise those peaches and we'll send you back to Oklahoma." At first I wondered how he knew I was from Oklahoma, but after I heard him holler some more, I realized that he said the same thing to everyone. It didn't matter whether you were from Texas or Missouri or Louisiana, he still threatened to send you to Oklahoma. The way he said *Oklahoma* made me feel bad. To me Oklahoma meant home and open, uncrowded sky, but he made it sound worse than a hog wallow.

I was proud of how fast Lester worked. Being that he is a skinny kid with long arms, he has a great reach. He was working a couple of trees over from me and jumping as fast as spit on a griddle. That's why I was surprised when I heard the foreman shout, "Hey, you boy," and it was Lester who called, "Me, sir?"

"What you doing with peach juice running down your chin?" the man continued, and Lester came back with the same, "Me, sir?"

The next thing I knew the man was ripping into Lester about being a little pig and eating up all the profits of the farm. He went on and on, making it sound like Lester's eating one peach would put this operation on the verge of bankruptcy.

I'd just started down the ladder when I heard Daddy's voice say, "You leave that boy alone." I scooted over as fast as I could. Knowing Daddy's temper, I could see him coldcocking that foreman and getting us all in big trouble. The foreman was just turning around and asking Daddy to repeat what he had just said when I pulled up beside Lester. I pointed to my little brother to distract him. "What he means to say," I interrupted, "is that Lester here promises he won't eat no more peaches. Right, Lester?"

When Lester nodded, the foreman cooled down. "All right then," he said, giving Lester a little cuff on the shoulder and telling him to get back up the ladder.

Daddy curled up his fist when he saw the man touch Lester, but I stepped toward Daddy and held out my hand, asking if his fingers were getting all crampy, too. Daddy grinned then, knowing my meaning, and he said that we'd best get back to picking.

At the end of the day we were paid cash money at the rate of five cents per box. I expected the man to at least thank us for coming, but the only thing he said was, "Same time tomorrow." No thank-you or have an nice evening, only, "Same time tomorrow."

After we pulled out of the driveway and started down the road, I reached in my pocket and handed Lester a peach. "You snuck one, C.J.?" Lester's eyes got big. I nodded and told him I wasn't about to let the foreman treat him that way. When Lester decided he would wait and share his peach with the younguns, Daddy grinned and said, "They've already been taken care of," as he pulled out three small peaches of his own.

June 29

We finished our second day of picking peaches. My bones are aching from all the climbing and stretching, but it's a good feeling to finally be making money.

Olive joined us today, and she did just fine. Dalton and Belle wanted to come, too, but Mother said she wasn't about to allow her babies to become fruit pickers.

June 30

Though it's Sunday, there are no days off when the fruit is ripe. A bunch more workers showed up at the orchard today, and the foreman announced that he was lowering the price to three cents per box. When an older fellow grumbled that it wasn't fair, the foreman walked up to him and asked if he was looking for trouble. "You ain't one of them labor-organizing Reds, is you?" he said. The fellow shook his head, but a couple of other men threw down their sacks and walked off.

July 1

Now that we have a little money, we went into town and bought some groceries. The hardest thing about shopping around here is driving past all the fruit and vegetables lying just a few steps from the road. I know these big farms wouldn't miss a tomato or a melon, but the guards on patrol are itching to pinch you. That leaves us no choice but to pay the high prices.

Today I noticed that California folks don't look you in the eye when they talk to you. Unlike the people back home, they gander at their shoes, or they look right past you at the walls or the ceiling, like you aren't even there. I wonder why that is.

July 5

The work at the peach orchard is near over now. I can't say I mind being finished. Now that they've lowered the price it barely pays for our gas to drive out to the farm and back. The trouble is, three cents is better than nothing.

July 6

Daddy had to replace the radiator in our truck today. Clem gave us a ride to a junkyard and helped us pull a used radiator off a '24 Model T. Not only did it cost us three dollars, but we also lost out on a whole day of picking. Clem gave up a day of work, too, just to help us. That sure was kind of him.

Now that we know most of the folks around camp, I've found that everyone looks out for one another. We let each other know where work is to be had and which farms to avoid. And we warn everyone if we hear that the police or sheriffs are coming. Word got out that some fellows were coming around tonight, so we were ready. Two cars of drunk high school boys pulled into camp after supper, but when they saw that every man in camp was sitting with a tire iron or a wrench balanced on his knee, they drove off real quick.

July 8

I've figured out why the local people don't like to look us Okies in the eye. The farmers out here need us to be around when the crops are ready for picking. The problem is that picking time only lasts a few weeks. Between crops they want us to be invisible. That's a hard trick for a man who needs to breathe and eat. Sometimes I feel like I'm trapped inside a steel cocoon.

July 10

We are still looking for another place to work. Everywhere we go it's the same story. There's a passel of workers but only a handful of jobs.

Daddy and Lester and I worked two days in a melon field, but when we came back on the third day, they had hired other fellows to take our place. I see why they call vegetable picking "stoop labor" — it's ten hours straight of squatting and lifting. Since Lester is lower to the ground than Daddy or me, he was a little quicker at melon picking. That made him real proud.

July 11

I just found out that Mother has planted a secret garden. Before the younguns woke up this morning she showed me a tiny patch of ground beyond the camp that she's tilled up. She says a few of the other women have done the same thing, but they are careful to keep their plots hidden. Mother walks a different way each time, so as to not make a trail, and she's left tall weeds on all sides. She's planted beans, cucumbers, potatoes, and a few tomato plants. I helped her carry water and promised not to tell the younguns, as they would be bragging to everyone.

July 12

We went shopping in town again today. We can't afford to go to a movie but on our way back to the truck I peeked into the lobby of the motion picture theater. I was admiring the fancy brass posts and velvet cording when I saw a sign on the wall that read NEGROES AND OKIES UPSTAIRS.

I turned around real quick and bumped into Olive, who was trying to get a look of her own. "What's wrong?" she asked, noticing how red my face was.

Before Olive could say anything more, Daddy, who had seen the sign, too, took her by the arm and led her away. Though I could tell Daddy was roaring mad, he kept calm. "Your brother was just checking to see if there were any Ginger Rogers and Fred Astaire posters in there for you to look at," he said, "and they don't have nothing but pictures of Errol Flynn."

"Errol Flynn!" Olive moaned.

Without meaning to, Daddy had picked the name of one of Olive's favorite actors.

July 15

We've found work in an apricot orchard. Everyone in the family except Belle and Dalton is picking. The foreman says Dalton is plenty old to work off a ladder, but Mother thinks otherwise. We all have to keep an eye on Belle, because she tends to wander off. Today I noticed for the first time that Belle's hair is darkening. It looks like she is going to take after Mother.

July 20

We had just got back from a full day in the orchard when two police cars screamed into camp. The cops stepped right out, but instead of strutting past the shacks with their clubs like they did last time, they split up and swung out into the brush.

I knew what was happening right away. A minute later one of the deputies hollered, "Look what we got here, Slim. Somebody's pretending to be a farmer."

Though Mother tugged on my arm and whispered for me to stay put, I walked over to the edge of the clearing. The deputy yelled even louder now. "I think these Okie folk need a lesson in thinning out their crops."

I watched as he trampled Mother's tomato vines. With a mean grin he made sure he stomped every plant. Then he took his boot heel and smashed the green tomatoes into the ground.

As he was finishing, the third fellow yelled that he'd found another garden. I watched them tromp off through the weeds.

"I wish they'd fall and break their necks," I said to Mother. "Why would they ever do something like that?"

To my surprise, there wasn't any anger in Mother's face, only pity. She told me that when folks is raised wrong, they can't help acting mean. Then she smiled. I didn't know what she was smiling about until the lawmen drove off. She fetched three tomatoes the deputy had missed and cleaned them off good. Then with the younguns all watching hungry-mouthed, she got out her skillet and cooked up a big mess of fried green tomatoes.

August 1

We are working a plum orchard at a smaller farm. The pay is a little better here, and the folks are a lot more respectful of their help. It's too bad we didn't find this place sooner, 'cause they harvest a whole succession of crops here, starting with special varieties of early peaches and continuing all summer. Best of all, they don't object if we take a little fruit now and then. Poor Lester ate so many plums the first day that he got a bad bellyache, and now he can't hardly look at a plum.

To save gas money, we've moved to a squatters' camp near the farm. Though it smells a little better than Hooverville, the sun is a lot worse. We buy our drinking water by the bucket at a gas station and dip our wash water from an irrigation ditch.

We've been working with an old fellow named Grady who's been following the crops up the San Joaquin Valley most of his life. He said things have changed in recent years. There used to be lots of smaller family farms like this one that took good care of their help and welcomed them back each year.

He claims that the biggest places — "factory farms," he calls them — "aren't even owned by people." When Daddy argued that every place had to be owned by someone, Grady said, "Nope. It's not a man no more, only banks and big corporations, and they's all drove by the almighty dollar."

August 8

I'm almost as sick of looking at plums as Lester is, but we've finally managed to save a few nickels. We may have a shot at paying off the taxes on our farm after all.

August 16

Will Rogers died yesterday in a plane crash up in Alaska. Everyone is talking about it. Other than Jim Thorpe, Mr. Rogers was about the most famous Oklahoman ever. He was known for saying that he had never met a man he didn't like, and by the way folks are talking, there wasn't anyone — Californians included — who didn't like him.

August 17

Mother and Daddy have been talking a lot about Will Rogers lately. It's almost as if we've lost a friend of the family.

Grandpa used to like Mr. Rogers, too. He especially enjoyed when Will Rogers made fun of politicians and said things like America is the only nation in history where the people go to the poorhouse in automobiles. And Grandpa thought Mr. Rogers was dead right when he said the only thing the folks in Washington ever improve is taxes.

When I get sad about Grandpa, I take out my gold piece. The shine of it reminds me of the old dugout behind our house. After all the good years that Grandpa had on the prairie, I feel bad that he had to suffer through the coming of the dust storms. That coin gives me hope that we can work our way home if we don't give up.

August 19

We've switched over to picking apples on the same farm. They say most of the apple orchards are farther north, so we're lucky they have one here. Apples don't bruise so easy, and they don't attract so many bees or have the oversweet smell of peaches that makes me dizzy when I have to work on an empty stomach.

August 25

Daddy and I talked to a bindle stiff who was hired on as an apple picker. He's working his way up to Salinas, and he happened to be in Los Angeles on the day of Will Rogers's funeral. He said 10,000 people were there, including every single movie star in the whole world.

I wonder if anyone at that funeral called Mr. Rogers an Okie.

September 9

Now that autumn is getting close, Mother feels bad that we aren't in school. She wants to look into enrolling us, but we can't afford to give up the money we kids are making. I never thought it would come down to choosing between schooling and starving, but that's where we're at.

September 14

This afternoon when we drove to the store, I saw one of the saddest sights I have ever laid eyes on. On a big truck farm they'd piled up a mound of leftover vegetables — dented melons, tomatoes that had fallen off the vines, and the like. Hundreds of poor folks, including us, would've carried that stuff off for free. Instead they poured fuel oil on top and set it on fire.

Burning up food like that is pure meanness. They guard their almonds just as close. The other day a fellow from our camp was arrested at a farm when he tried to gather up some windfall almonds. His baby has pellagra, his wife has got tuberculosis, and to top it all off, now he's going to jail.

If those big farms keep treating people as bad as they have, union organizers will be the least of their worries. It's only a matter of time before someone starts fighting back. A man can stand just so much.

October 15

The fruit ran out, but we've found work picking cotton. We get paid only 75 cents per 100 pounds, but with the whole family working we should be able to save enough to finish off our tax bill. The only thing that makes me nervous is how light cotton is. It must take a heap of cotton bolls to add up to 100 pounds.

The manager of the farm has rented us a shack for $12 a month with the understanding that we keep four workers in the field all day long. The manager has it figured that if each person picks 200 pounds per day, every shack will produce 800 pounds. Lester and Daddy and I plan on working full time while Mother and Olive switch off watching Dalton and Belle. Though some folks let children as young as six out in the fields, Mother will not allow that. I am looking forward to working on my own two feet for a change instead of dangling from a ladder with branches slapping me in the face.

October 16

Cotton picking is not as easy as I hoped it would be. It wouldn't be so bad if we could get started in the cool of the morning, but the manager makes us wait until the dew is burned away. By the time the cotton bolls are dry, the sun is blazing.

After our first hour in the field, nobody was smiling. We drag long sacks behind us as we work. Though the sacks are light when they're empty, they pull on your shoulder good as they get full. I've noticed that folks who've done a lot of cotton picking tend to walk crooked and stooped over. After I put in a few more ten-hour days, I figure I'll have trouble walking straight, too.

The worst part is my hands. Not only do they get cramped like they do from fruit picking, but they also get cut. The cotton fibers and the prickly leaves can bloody your hands in a hurry. Daddy and I have calluses, but Olive's hands got ripped up bad. At lunchtime Mother took a turn and let Olive rest — if you call keeping track of that little live wire Belle a rest!

It's tricky to pick fast and clean. Before you climb up and dump your cotton into the farm wagon, the scalers weigh your sack on a big tripod scale. They check to make sure you haven't grabbed up twigs and leaves along with the cotton. The first time they weighed Lester's cotton, they adjusted his total down. He was ready to cry until I told him that it would take us all a while to catch on to a new line of work like this.

The truth is, even if I practice, I don't know that I'll ever get up to 200 pounds a day. For a whole day's work I made $1.10, Daddy $1.25, Olive and Mother $.95, and Lester only $.65.

Mother is patching up some gloves for Olive to wear tomorrow.

October 18

I finally have a table to write on. Even if it's a shaky old thing built from a chipped-up signboard and fence-picket legs, it makes a lot steadier desk than my knee. The problem is I'm too tuckered out to think let alone write any more.

October 21

I'm getting so I can walk those rows in my sleep. Walk and pick. Walk and pick. Climb the ladder on that slat-sided wagon and empty your sack onto the big hill of cotton. Walk and pick.

To keep my mind from shutting down, I like to think back on the prairie: the look of the wheat at harvesttime, the sound of a thunderhead rumbling in, the smell of the autumn earth. I also like to remember my favorite books, like Zane Grey's *Riders of the Purple Sage,* one chapter at a time.

October 25

Olive's hands have toughened up and she is doing her full share in the field. But I feel sorry for Lester. He's gotten to be one of the fastest pickers in the camp, but his nerves are suffering. Last night I heard him moving on the floor beside me. When I looked up, his hands were outside his blanket and plucking at the air, like he was picking imaginary cotton bolls in his sleep.

October 26

Our pay isn't coming out as good as we thought it would. Not only do we have to pay rent for our shack, which is nothing more than four crooked walls and a roof that is so leaky that dots of sunlight show through, but we also have to pay for what they call "utilities." Utilities means we can tap water from a spigot in the middle of the camp for five cents per bucket. We get to use the outhouse for free, but it's full up to the top and makes me gag so bad that I can't hardly go to the toilet. There's one shower stall for the 200 people in our half of the camp, but the lines are so long, it's easier to sponge ourselves off from pails that Lester and I fetch from the irrigation ditch.

November 4

Daddy swears that these cotton scales are rigged to weigh light. He knows we are picking faster than we used to, but our totals don't seem to be going up.

He says that instead of beating up bindle stiffs and raiding ditch bank camps, the sheriffs should be checking to see that the weighing equipment in these cotton camps is legal.

November 11

When it rains we can't pick cotton, so the manager hires us sometimes for other jobs around the farm. Today Daddy and I got paid a quarter each for digging a new hole for the outhouse. Shoveling soupy dirt clods is miserable in the rain, but we can't afford to go a day without working. We got muddied up so bad that Belle asked if we had been playing in a pigpen.

December 11

I can't believe a whole month has passed since I wrote last, but how many ways can I describe what it's like to stuff a cotton sack or shovel mud?

December 14

I finally saw something new today. Fog. And by fog I don't mean the airy stuff that we get back home, I mean a solid sheet of white. When I stepped outside this morning, I couldn't even see our truck, which is parked only a couple of paces from our door.

Belle and Dalton and some of the other younguns had a lark playing hide-and-seek. Mother is worried that they'll trip and fall into a ditch or a well. I'm afraid that they are both getting a little unruly, especially Belle, who's been downright sassy.

December 15

Daddy sat us all down tonight after a dinner of lard-fried bread. He said we had a choice to make. We'd saved exactly $31.50 from our summer and fall wages. Since that included money that me and Olive and Lester had contributed through our picking, Daddy said we should be a part of the decision making.

Then he laid it out straight. We could either have Christmas or send $29.75 back to the county treasurer, J.M. Enlow, to pay the tax bill due on our farm. At the thought of missing Christmas, Lester's head went down, and Olive flinched, but neither said a word. Finally Olive spoke up. "Paying our taxes is our only hope of ever getting home, right?" she asked.

When Daddy nodded, she surprised me by saying, "Then that's what we need to do."

Daddy and Mother looked toward me and Lester. When we agreed, I could tell that they were proud that our love of the land hadn't been beat out of us by the hard times we'd been having in California. Daddy was just opening his mouth to thank us when Olive piped up again. Here we go, I thought, the real Olive is coming out and she's going to change her mind. But she surprised me again by saying that if we had any money left over, it was only right that we get Dalton and Belle presents, 'cause they were the littlest.

December 19

Dalton has caught a bad cold. Mother mixed up a liniment of mustard, eggs, onions, kerosene, and turpentine and rubbed it on his chest. For once I am glad that we are sleeping in a leaky shack. If our quarters were any tighter, the smell would choke us all off.

A baby died in one of the cabins, and since the family

doesn't have any money for a funeral, everyone is pitching in a dime.

December 25

The fog continues off and on. Sometimes it burns off by ten, and other times it lays in for a day or two at a time.

Though we older kids went without presents today, Dalton got a new cap, and Mother sewed up a sackcloth dress with a pretty bow for Belle. Daddy did buy us all a bag of nuts and a fruitcake, which was a nice surprise.

January 1, 1936

The one good thing about having as rough a time as we did last year is that things can't hardly get any worse this year.

Though the cotton picking is down to nothing, the owner of the farm will let us stay on until we can find somewhere else to go. Everyone says that we'd better sit tight, because jobs are scarce between now and planting time.

That advice may be good, but I heard Mother and Daddy talking it over last night after they thought we were all asleep. They are worried about the $12 a month we have to pay for rent. What about money for food? I wanted to ask, but I guess they need to make sure we have a roof over our heads first. I sure hope we don't have to go back and live in that Hooverville ditch bank camp now that the rainy season is here.

January 4

It's either rain or fog nearly every day. Sometimes we get little spats of sleet between. The temperature's dropped to freezing or colder every night this week. Mother wraps blankets over the shoulders of the younguns, and they huddle close to the little tin stove, but there's no real warmth in this drafty shack.

January 11

Daddy and Lester and I have been doing small jobs around the farm: ditching, fencing, clearing brush. The money doesn't amount to much, but we need to scrape by somehow between now and when the first crops come in.

Now that we are only working one day out of three, I've had lots of time to write in this journal, but I've lost my fire for writing. If we have to stay in this muddy cotton camp much longer, I'm afraid I'll lose my fire for just about everything. I used to dream about food a lot when I went to bed hungry. I'd picture an oven-roasted chicken or big slab of steak still sizzling, but lately my dreams have turned to washed-out pictures, as empty as the winter sky.

January 18

We drove to town this afternoon to buy groceries. Though we burn up gas driving all that way, the prices are just too high at the little store they keep on the farm. Daddy jokes that if we shopped there all the time, we'd have to give up eating altogether.

The sun was out for the first time in quite a few days, so we were all in a good mood. We bought the small sack of things that we needed and headed back toward our truck.

Olive and Belle, who were walking together, hung behind us a little bit and stopped to look in a store window. I heard a voice yell, "Get clear of that window, you no good Okie trash."

I turned and saw that Belle had one finger on the glass and was pointing out something to Olive. The storekeeper had stepped through his doorway by then, and he shouted even louder, "I said get, you no-goods. I just washed that window."

Daddy wheeled around and ran back to the girls. Belle was crying so loud that I don't think Daddy heard Mother shout for him to stop. But it was too late anyway. Daddy punched that fellow so hard that he flew backward into his store and crashed into a hat rack as he fell.

Next thing I knew a fellow across the street was yelling, "Police, police." Only a few minutes later Daddy was handcuffed, shoved into the back of a squad car, and gone.

January 20

Mother and I visited Daddy in jail this afternoon. As the guard led us back to the cell, he mumbled something that sounded like, "More shiftless Okies to see the same," but I wasn't sure if I heard it right.

I was about to say something when Mother touched my shoulder. "Easy, C.J.," she said. "Losing one man's enough."

Though Daddy is not sorry that he hit the man, he is very sorry that he's brought trouble on us all. "It'll be up to you, C.J.," he said, "to see that the family makes it through."

Normally I'd be proud if Mother called me a man and Daddy told me the family was depending on me, but at this moment I am scared flat out of my wits. I just wish there was some way to take us all back to Oklahoma and start up the rains and make this misery go away.

January 23

Daddy had his trial today. We took our seats toward the middle of the mostly empty courtroom, and I settled in for a long wait. I expected there'd be testimony and witnesses and speeches. Instead, it was all over in a couple of minutes flat.

The judge asked Daddy if he had hit the man. Daddy nodded and said, "Yes, sir."

"Thirty days or thirty dollars?" the judge asked. He didn't bother to ask Daddy for an explanation of why he had punched that fellow. I was ready to stand up and say that my daddy is a well-respected man, and that someone should be allowed to speak in his behalf. But before I could even flex my knees, Daddy said he didn't have thirty dollars and the judge dropped his gavel and called the next case forward.

We all walked out of that courtroom shuffling mighty slow. What would we do to support ourselves for the next month? It didn't help matters that Belle kept asking why Daddy wasn't coming home with us. I made up a lie and told her that Daddy would be going off to work at another job for a while.

That set Belle off asking what kind of job and where was it and why couldn't we go with him. I was trying to think of a way to hush her when a man walked up to Mother. He excused himself for interrupting but asked if he could speak with us. Mother was hesitant at first — I could tell she was wondering if he was a lawman — but he was such a gentle, soft-spoken fellow that she let him go on. His name was Tom Collins and he was in the courthouse on business when he happened to overhear our case. He said he was the manager of a brand-new federal camp for farm laborers south of Bakersfield, and he invited us to come and stay there.

Mother told him we didn't have hardly any rent money. When he said they charged only $1 a week, I couldn't keep quiet any longer.

"A dollar a week!" I blurted out. He thought I was mad at him until I explained that we were paying three times that amount to stay in a rickety cotton-camp shack.

Then he smiled and told us the best part of all. If the dollar was hard to come by, we could do jobs around the camp instead of making cash payments.

“How do we get to this camp?” Mother asked with a smile.

January 24

“Thirty days or thirty dollars?” I keep hearing that judge’s voice echoing over and over. I sure hope Daddy is doing okay.

Tomorrow we are moving to the camp near Arvin that Mr. Collins told us about.

January 25

We got officially accepted into the Arvin Federal Camp and moved in this afternoon. At first I didn’t like the look of the place. It had a fence all around it, and there were tents in rows and buildings with metal roofs that gave it the look of a prison. That made me think of Daddy, locked up and alone.

However, Mr. Collins explained that the fences were not for keeping people locked up inside, but for stopping sheriffs who didn’t have search warrants and wanted to pick on people.

My ears perked up when I heard that. How nice it would be to relax and not have to worry about a lawman strutting up and sticking his pistol in your face for no reason.

January 26

Weedpatch — that's the name everyone uses for this place instead of Arvin Federal Camp — sure is a big change from that muddy cotton camp! I have never seen an operation that is so clean and orderly. The living quarters include wall tents and cabins, which a construction crew is still building. About a dozen families are living here right now, but there will be room for four times that many when the camp is finished.

Though we only got a tent, it has a kitchen with hot and cold running water — that's fancier than back home! — and an outdoor pantry. The camp also has shower baths, a utility room, and a community building. They plan to add a clinic, a nursery, and a grease rack for working on cars. My favorite building is the library. You can barely turn around inside, and most of the books get checked out the minute they come in, but there are plenty of newspapers and magazines to read. I put my name on the reserve list for a Zane Grey called *Wanderer of the Wasteland*.

January 27

It is an indescribable pleasure to take a bath without having to lug the water in buckets and heat it on a stove. When I stand under the shower and let that warm water pour over me, I am afraid to close my eyes lest this all prove to be a dream and I wake up back in Hooverville.

January 28

I am learning something new about Weedpatch Camp every day. The whole place is run by committee. Mr. Collins believes in democracy, and he thinks that people should make the decisions that affect their lives. A Campers Committee is in charge of discipline and law and order. There's also a Recreation and Entertainment Committee, a Child Welfare Committee, and a Good Neighbor Committee that collects and repairs old clothes. Teachers will be coming in to give classes on different practical subjects, too, like nutrition and hygiene, child care, butchering, and woodworking.

Mr. Collins said that when the camp is finished, they plan on having enough tents and cabins to hold three or four hundred people. Some day they may have to call this place Weedpatch City.

January 29

We are down to our last nickel. Though we can work off our rent, we still need to eat. Lester and I have looked for work around Arvin and Lamont, but nothing has turned up.

I sure miss Daddy.

January 30

Now that we have a permanent address, I've written to Jed Roberts and Aunt Ruby and asked how things are going back in the Panhandle. A powerful lonesomeness for Oklahoma still hits me some days. And the hurt is just as bad as it was on the day we left the farm. Little things can set it off, like the scent of winter grass greening in a patch of sun beside a building or the look of a car that I catch out of the corner of my eye and think, Hey, that's Bobby Young, before I turn and realize that Bobby and Boise City are more than a thousand miles away. It happened again just this morning. I was lying in my quilt half asleep. All of a sudden the smell of side pork sizzling next door brought a picture of a prairie sunrise flashing back so clear in my mind that I was startled to wake up in a Weedpatch tent.

February 1

Mr. Collins lets folks gather round and listen to his radio. *Fibber McGee and Molly* is still going strong. Mr. Collins favors news programs, especially when they have stories about the president's wife, Eleanor Roosevelt. She is campaigning hard for the government to guarantee everyone jobs, food, and medicine.

Tonight we are having musical entertainment and a dance. A bunch of folks have been practicing with a harmonica, fiddle, banjo, spoons, and a washboard. Olive is going to sing with them.

February 5

Mr. Collins has lined up some fence repair work for me at a farm that's only two miles down the road. It doesn't pay much, but at least we can buy some groceries. I won't have to drive the truck, either, which will save us gas.

I asked Mr. Collins if Lester could work, too, but he told me that Lester and Olive should probably go to school. Mother agreed with him, and they are both starting on Monday.

February 6

I finally got *Wanderer of the Wasteland* from the library.

February 9

The temperature creeps up into the sixties most days, and it looks like spring will soon be in full bloom.

Some of us boys have been playing baseball in the evening. After a hard day of shoveling and fence-post pounding, it feels good to get out and run. My fielding is a bit rusty, but I'm already hitting solid.

Mr. Collins plays ball with us when he has time. Unlike most adults who boss kids around whenever they join in a game, he sits back and waits to be invited. He insists we do our own umpiring and settle disputes on our own. Mr. Collins has real quick hands and can snag a line drive barehanded without even flinching.

February 10

Lester and Olive came home mad from their first day of school. They both claim that their teachers barely talked to them. Lester said he wasn't allowed to have books, and he had to sit on the floor in the back of the room all by himself.

Mother said she didn't want to hear any complaining and reminded them of the old saying: "Smile and the world smiles with you. Cry and you cry alone."

February 12

Mr. Timmons — he's the farmer I'm working for — has switched me over to helping prepare the fields for planting. So far he's been a fair man.

I finished *Wanderer of the Wasteland* tonight. It was the longest book I've ever read — 419 pages!

February 13

Aunt Ruby wrote back. She was happy to tell us that she is in good health and that the fields have finally got a little moisture this winter. Since she knows the younguns like dinosaurs, she sent us some clippings from the *Boise City News,* telling more details of the big dinosaur that was discovered last spring. Scientists from the University of Oklahoma have now uncovered a nearly complete skeleton. When I read the part out loud about the rib bones being five feet long, Lester's eyes got big and he asked me to please repeat that. When Belle saw the picture that they'd drawn of the dinosaur, she said she wasn't ever going back to Cimarron County if there were critters that big roaming around. I tried explaining that the dinosaurs were long gone, but she kept asking where they'd got the picture then.

February 16

According to a *Newsweek* magazine in our library, the Californians are making their already sad record for friendliness even worse. Los Angeles police chief, James Davis, has taken it on himself to set up roadblocks at every border crossing to stop Dust Bowl migrants from entering the state. He's stationed 150 L.A. police officers from Arizona to Oregon. They are calling his operation a "Bum Blockade."

Mr. Collins says that Davis is breaking the law, and that a group called the Civil Liberties Union will stop him. In the meantime, I sure feel sorry for all those folks who are stuck at the border. It's a sorry day when the men who are supposed to be enforcing the laws are ignoring them.

February 17

I talked with Mr. Collins again tonight. Though he is a quiet man, he has very strong opinions. He told me that if I thought Chief Davis was bad, there is a Senator Phillips in California who is even worse. He called Phillips "a mean-spirited fascist" and an admirer of a German bully named Hitler.

Then Mr. Collins stopped and said he was sorry for "getting up on his high horse" and preaching at me. He explained that he was sad because he thought California needed a politician with the courage of someone like President Lincoln (his birthday was just last Wednesday), but he didn't see anyone stepping forward.

February 18

I finally got a letter from Jed Roberts today. He was glad to report, same as Aunt Ruby had, that the rains are slowly coming back. He says his daddy figures it will take a long time yet for the land to green up like it once was, but they have a good chance to make a fair wheat crop this year.

Jed rides over to our place and checks on it once in a

while. He says our farm is "ready and waiting" for us to come back. Since I'd told him we planned on keeping up our taxes, he let me know that we have a new treasurer in Boise City, Elenora Bourk, who will be collecting this year's payments. As a P.S. he added that he thought of me the other day when the barn door blew open and cracked him in the head. To show that he still had a sense of humor he signed his name Calamity Jed.

February 19

Aunt Ruby sent us a whole box of books! There's a pile of picture books for the younguns and a few westerns for me and Lester. She said that after we are finished we should donate them to the camp library.

February 20

We picked Daddy up at the jail this morning. Counting credit for the days served before his trial, today came out to exactly thirty days.

Though Daddy is normally a quiet fellow, he was more quiet than ever on the drive back. I didn't expect him to apologize for doing something he had to do, but I thought he'd at least talk about how much he missed us or how lonely he'd been.

February 22

Daddy's silence worries me. He hardly even talks to Belle, and she missed him a whole lot. I wonder if something bad happened to him in prison that he doesn't want to talk about.

February 29

This past week Mr. Collins has been giving groups of growers and local politicians tours of the camp. Collins says he's doing it to show the people that we aren't a bunch of agitators in here, just plain folks who are doing our best to earn an honest living.

I know he means well, but when those people gawk at us, I feel like I'm some sort of experimental stock breed that's being showed off at the county fair.

Daddy finally pepped up and made a joke. He said that if we charged those tour folks admission, we wouldn't have to worry about finding any more jobs. But the fact is we need jobs bad. I finished up at Timmons' farm last week, and there's nothing else available. Word is cotton planting will start soon.

March 1

Daddy came out of his silence in full force today. It was all brought on by some church folk.

There are a few different Sunday groups here in camp that try to get folks to join in their services. Mother divides them into two groups: the "regular" and the "other." The regular are those who preach normal like our minister back home did. The others are a mix of faith healers and holy rollers who believe that a church service isn't any good if it don't get you to feeling the spirit so strong that you jump and holler.

Well, this morning one of the faith-healer types cornered Mother and tried to talk her into coming over to their meeting. Mother was polite, but the lady went on and on like she was trying to talk her to death.

Suddenly Daddy stood up. "You stop right there, Ma'am," he said, looking her straight in the eye. "It ain't right of you to bother us about going to your church when we don't pester you to go to ours."

She puffed up like she was ready to start in again, but Daddy kept right on preaching tolerance to her until he'd walked her two cabins down the street and out of our hair.

When Daddy came back, he was smiling for the first time since his arrest. Mother thanked him, and then he surprised us all by saying, "I need to remind myself that even if I am a convict, there's no reason why I can't talk to folks when I need to."

Mother and I both tried to tell him that he was no convict just because he'd hit a man who'd been disrespecting his daughters. Mother even told him that the sassy shopkeeper only got half of what he deserved, but Daddy wouldn't listen.

"I've got a record now, Cleo," he said, "and it's a-goin' to follow me the rest of my days."

March 2

Knowing the reason for Daddy's silence pains me even more than his not talking did. I hope that time will heal his hurt.

Our food money is down to nothing again, but now that the dandelions have greened up, we can at least have salad. It helps that Lester and I are doing extra work around camp, and we're getting paid with a cupful of flour and teaspoon of lard.

March 3

We heard that the peas down in the Imperial Valley will be ready for harvesting next month. Daddy has talked about heading down that way, but we hate to give up our spot in Weepatch. It shouldn't be too long before the field work begins around here.

After the "regular" camp church service yesterday, Daddy talked to a fellow who said there was work digging ditches by a town called Wheeler Ridge. So he and I headed down Route 99 this morning to scout things out. Just this side of a bridge we came across a brand-new Cadillac stalled beside the road. Daddy wasn't sure whether he should stop, but it was so chilly and wet that he felt sorry for the fellow. The hood was up, and the man was staring at the engine and scratching his head.

Daddy pulled over to the shoulder and called, "Need some help?"

The man, who was wearing a fancy suit and tie, looked at Daddy and our run-down ole truck and frowned. I could tell that he was ready to send us on our way, but when he glanced up and down the highway and saw that there were no cars coming in either direction, he nodded and said, "She quit dead on me."

Daddy and I got out of our truck. "A Fleetwood V-16, eh?" Daddy admired it as he walked toward the long, low-slung car. The hood of the Cadillac was nearly as long as our whole truck, and the slender chrome grill was topped by a hood ornament of a flying lady.

The man nodded again, but this time he was smiling. "I can tell you appreciate a fine automobile. This same model is a favorite of Marlene Dietrich, who just happens to be a personal friend of mine."

Daddy never did give a lick about actresses, and he showed it by sticking his head under the hood while the fellow was still blabbing. I peeked over Daddy's shoulder at the gigantic sixteen-cylinder engine of the Cadillac. I'd seen pictures of these cars, but I'd never got a close look at one. Every square inch of the engine compartment was enameled, polished, and chromed. All the wires and hoses were hidden under fancy metal plates, and the valve covers were as long as my arms. It took just a few streaks of sun peeking through the mottled gray sky behind us to shine off that chrome and make me squint.

As Daddy tinkered under the hood, the man kept talking about Marlene Dietrich. He bragged about how often he saw her, how her personal chauffeur had mink collars on his uniform and carried two .45-caliber pistols on his belt, and how Miss Dietrich liked these cars so much that she had ordered a second V-16 Cadillac town car, which she was going to pick up over in London.

I was curious to hear more, but Daddy wanted to get

right down to the mechanical problem. He asked the man a quick string of questions: How long ago had the engine quit? How did it sound right before it cut out? Had it ever acted like that before? And so on. The fellow answered politely enough, but at the same time, he kept glancing up and down the road, like he was hoping that somebody else would come along.

Daddy had me fetch a pair of pliers and a screwdriver out of the truck. After working for no more than two minutes, he said, "Let's give her a try."

When the engine fired right up, the man was astonished. "What on earth did you do?" he asked.

Daddy explained that the coil wire had come loose, and that all he'd needed to do was tighten it down. The man shook Daddy's hand and kept talking as fast as ever. He said he owned a car dealership down in Los Angeles. Daddy nodded, but it was clear that he was as unimpressed by this news as he'd been by the man's movie star friends. Daddy turned to walk back to our truck, but the man wouldn't let him go until he explained that he was always in the market for skilled mechanics, and that if Daddy ever decided to move to L.A., he would hire him in a minute.

Before the man drove off, he handed Daddy a business card and told him to please give him a call. We climbed into our truck, and Daddy went to throw the card out the window. He was sure the man was only joshing him — "like all fast talkers do," he said. But I told him we'd best not litter, and I stuck that card in my pocket right next to my lucky gold piece.

By the time we found the ranch, it was the same ole story. "If you'd only been here yesterday," the foreman said.

On the way home I asked Daddy if he planned on calling that car dealer, but he ignored my question altogether. Scanning the sky to the west, he said, "Looks like rain could be rolling in."

I decided that my only hope was to show the card to Mother and see if she could talk him into calling.

March 4

Daddy was ready to box my ears when he found out I'd told Mother about the car dealer. She told Daddy it wouldn't hurt none for him to call that number one time, but Daddy said he wasn't about to play the fool and waste money telephoning someone "who just plans on having a laugh at a dumb Okie."

I'd never heard Daddy use the word *Okie* before. A year ago there wasn't a prouder man in the Panhandle, but I can see now that these tough times have taken him down a peg or two. As much as it hurts me to hear him run his own self down, it proves that if you call a man names long enough — even if they aren't true — he'll eventually become exactly what you want him to be.

March 7

Christmas has finally come to the Jacksons! Daddy was offered a mechanic's job, and we are moving to Los Angeles on Monday.

Mother worked on Daddy for the best part of the week before he finally gave in and called that car dealer. I had never seen Mother so feisty. After trying to word things politely, she finally laid down the law. "You and I are one thing, Lee Jackson," she said, "but if you're going to throw away a chance to help these children, then you can find yourself another woman to cook your corn bread."

Daddy's jaw went slack like he couldn't believe his ears. I think he knew Mother would never leave him, but the tone of her voice got his attention. Not long after that, he and Mother went off and made the phone call.

Not only did the car dealer want Daddy to come to work for him, but he also said that he had a friend who owned a trailer park down on the Coast Highway, and that we could rent a space there until we had time to find a house.

A house! Those words made the younguns so excited that they jumped up and down. We were as happy as that morning last June when we drove up the Tehachapi grade and looked out on the long green San Joaquin Valley for the first time. That was before we learned that sunshine and green can hide an ugliness that's worse than the most wicked duster.

I feel like a great weight has been lifted. After the months we've spent wandering from place to place, the hope of getting back to normal living is almost too much for me to believe.

March 14

We arrived in Los Angeles this afternoon. The country on both sides of Highway 99 was flat, brown, and barren, but just north of the city the land rises up toward the San Gabriel Mountains. The streets in L.A. are lined with more fancy houses and palm trees and flowers than I could ever imagine. I never knew there could be so many people packed into one place.

So many big cars whizzed past us that it made my head spin. Everybody was in such a rush that it was tricky navigating our pokey ole truck. Seeing how busy this place is, I can understand why Will Rogers once joked that L.A. was a nice place to live, but he sure wouldn't want to visit here.

The buzz of the traffic shocked everyone into silence except Olive. She would not shut her mouth. She'd been beside herself with excitement from the minute we crossed the Los Angeles County line, and now that we were finally in the city her mouth was going a mile a minute. Daddy tried to hush her, but she kept repeating, "I can't believe we're here."

We'd just joined up with Route 66 downtown when Olive let out a yell. Daddy hit the brakes, thinking she'd been hurt. It turned out that she'd only seen the famous HOLLYWOODLAND sign, and she was shouting for us to look. Daddy scoffed at the big white letters on the hillside. He said, "Least they could have done was line them letters up straight." Then Mother joined in and told Olive to quiet down and stop acting like Hollywood folks were the kings and queens of the world.

We had no trouble finding Bay District Motors Company, the Cadillac dealership were Daddy is supposed to work. It's just off Route 66 at 1115 Wilshire Boulevard. A salesman gave Daddy a mean sneer as he walked up to the big glass door in front. But when Daddy came back outside with the owner a few minutes later, that same fellow nodded and smiled at him real polite. The owner said hi to the whole family and thanked us for coming. Before we left, he gave us directions to the Miramar Trailer Park, and he told Daddy to show his card to the man at the gate.

Though Olive begged to take a detour through Hollywood so she could get a look at a movie star, Daddy said she could go to Hollywood herself when she signed her first movie contract. I thought his teasing might make Olive mad, but she took his comment to be serious and nodded to herself like she just might do that.

We followed Route 66 straight to the ocean. The highway runs through a town of pretty beach cottages called Santa Monica, then stops dead. I was taking my turn at the wheel, and I had to brake hard to keep from driving our truck right into the Pacific. A sign at the end of the pavement says

SANTA MONICA

66

END OF THE TRAIL

Just ahead stands a big palm tree. Beyond it there's a boardwalk, a long stretch of sand, and blue water that goes on forever.

As I studied the very last Route 66 sign in America, I couldn't help but think that our long journey from

Cimarron County had finally come to an end. This was as far west as we could go, unless we caught a boat, as Lester pointed out when he hollered, "How far you figure it is to Hawaii?"

March 15

When we got to the Miramar Trailer Park, the manager frowned at our rig until Daddy showed him the note from the car dealer. Then he nodded his head and said, "We've been expecting you."

He gave us a nice spot on the north end of the lot under the only shade tree. The park is just a narrow patch of ground with beach to the front and city to the rear. Most of the people are staying in travel trailers that look like tin boxes with beetle-backed roofs. The manager said we were welcome to set up a tarp for the night but asked if we would please take it down during the day. After supper we all took a walk along the beach. The most amazing thing in the neighborhood is a gigantic pier with a huge ballroom built at the very end. The ballroom has a domed roof and pointed towers, topped with flags, that make it look like the ocean palace of a maharaja.

After we got back to the trailer park, I still couldn't take my eyes off the Pacific. It's one thing to talk about the ocean, but quite another to see it for the first time. When I look at all that water, words like *endless, open, vast,* and *forever* come to mind, but every single description falls short of telling how truly grand it is. Like the prairie back home, the ocean has a way of humbling a fellow and putting him in his place. I'd like to bring every one of the puff-chested guards that strutted in front of our truck at those border crossings here. I'd bring every hotshot farm manager who tried telling us what a low kind of critter an Okie is down here, too. I'd stand them at the edge of the edge of the water at sunset and have them watch the sun sink into the Pacific. I wouldn't say a word as the sun got bigger by the minute and spilled red colors up the sky. Then just before the full dark, I'd turn to them and say, "There, you're not so big after all, are you?"

March 29

I've been hog-tied with homework lately and haven't had time to write. Though the houses were too expensive for us to rent, we moved into an apartment only a few blocks from Bay District Motors. Mother enrolled us in a brand-new school called Roosevelt, which has just been rebuilt because an earthquake damaged the old one.

It didn't take me long to find out that the secret to getting along with California kids is baseball. We play pickup games every recess and after school. Thanks to my practice up at Weedpatch, I smacked a line drive off the fence on only my second at-bat. If you can hit the ball hard, it doesn't matter if you're a movie producer's son or a farm boy from Oklahoma like me.

Daddy got his first paycheck yesterday. To celebrate he bought us a bag of oranges, and we went for a drive up the Coast Highway. On the way back we turned up Sunset Boulevard and rode past the gates of Will Rogers's estate. Later we stopped at a place called Inspiration Point. From there you can see the tall buildings of L.A. on one side and the Santa Monica Mountains on the other. Between the city and the mountains are a string of twisty, tree-lined canyons. Beyond it all lies the Pacific, stretching off wide and blue as far as you can see.

April 1

Jed Roberts wrote me a letter and said the prospects for the winter wheat crop still look good. He also said that he planted some prairie flowers on Grandpa's grave for me, and that he will let me know when they bloom. That was mighty nice of him.

April 7

I just noticed that I started keeping this journal exactly one year ago. It's hard for me to believe the miles we've put behind us since then. A trip to Boise City or Black Mesa used to be a long haul for me, but now I've traveled halfway across this country. And if I ever need reminding of the truth of my travels, all I have to do is open my journal. On every single page the mountains and deserts and orchards stand plain and pure.

As pretty as California is, and as much as Daddy likes working on those brand new Cadillacs and LaSalles, we all hope we will be moving back to the farm before too long. Daddy is saving up every penny he can from his job, and Lester and I plan to do field work this summer to help out. Though Mother insists that we need to have a whole year's taxes saved before we move back to Oklahoma, I figure by this time next year we should be heading east on Route 66.

Once I get home I'm going to bury my lucky gold piece by the corner of Grandpa's dugout right where I found it. Some folks might think that's a crazy thing to do, but I can't help feeling that this coin belongs in the ground.

Those dust storms ripped open the land and threw time out of balance. They uncovered things that were meant to stay buried. They uprooted hundreds of thousands of folks and drove them west.

Grandpa once told me that a farmer needs two things: patience and a knowledge of the land. If I'm patient, I know I'll see the prairie again.

Sometimes toward sundown when the noise of the city falls away, I can see the plains so clear in my mind that it's like I never left home. The same picture flashes blue and clear each time. The dust is gone just like in the old days, and the prairie is rippling green under an open Oklahoma sky. Though it may take some waiting for all that to come true again, I take a deep breath and smile every time I think of it. I know that the earth waits ready for the rains and for the healing that is sure to come.

But before I walk near that ole dugout, you can bet your bottom dollar that I'm going to keep my eyes peeled for rattlesnakes.

Epilogue

In August 1936 the Jackson family stopped by the Arvin Federal Camp to say hello to Tom Collins. Mr. Collins introduced C.J. and Lester to a writer named John Steinbeck, who was visiting the camp to do research for an article on migrant workers' living conditions. Mr. Steinbeck interviewed the boys, and they were both impressed with his concern for farm laborers.

After witnessing an L.A. celery strike in the spring of 1936 that was broken up by the brutal tactics of Chief Davis's deputies, C.J. and Lester did field work through that summer. By pooling their savings with Daddy's, the boys made it possible for the Jacksons to move back to Oklahoma in September. Everyone was eager to return to Cimarron County except for Olive, who decided to stay with a friend in Santa Monica and finish her schooling there.

Once the family paid the taxes on their farm, the still-depressed real estate values allowed them to buy another half section of grazing land. Though the rains soon returned, the dry years had left their mark on the plains, and it would take many decades of careful stewardship for the land to regain its former productivity.

C.J. forgot all about the author he had met at Weedpatch until 1939. As a senior in high school he picked up a copy of a new book called *The Grapes of Wrath* and saw that it was written by John Steinbeck. C.J. was amazed to discover that Mr. Steinbeck had written about a family who moved from Oklahoma to California and lived through many of the same things that the Jacksons had. Reading *The Grapes of Wrath* brought back many memories for C.J., and it inspired him to dedicate his life to helping the farmers of the plains avoid another Dust Bowl.

After getting degrees in agronomy and soil science from the University of Oklahoma, C.J. went to work for the United States Department of Agriculture. While employed as an extension agent and later as a field researcher and lecturer, C.J. worked hard to promote environmentally sound farming practices and prairie reclamation programs. Along with his career at the USDA, he wrote a popular series of western novels, under the pseudonym of Jack Slade.

C.J. married a girl from Woodward, Oklahoma, and they lived in several locations across the plains states during the years that he was doing his writing and research. They eventually had four children — three boys and one girl, who turned out to be the spitting image of C.J.'s mother.

When C.J. retired, he and his wife bought a small ranch near Black Mesa State Park. On his seventy-fifth birthday C.J. signed a pledge donating all future royalties from his novels to a conservation organization that is working to restore native prairie habitat.

The Jackson farm prospered as the country gradually pulled out of the Depression and the price of beef and grain rose. The increased demand for wheat during World War II allowed the Jacksons to make enough money to buy another section of land.

During World War II Lester went back to California and worked for the Douglas Aircraft Company. He was eventually promoted to project manager. After helping Mother and Daddy run the family farm, Dalton took over the operation in 1972, when his parents moved to an apartment in Boise City. Olive got the lead role in several plays while attending Santa Monica High School, but she eventually gave up on her Hollywood dreams and opened a beauty shop in Venice, California. Belle planned on spending her life in the Panhandle. However, when she was visiting Olive in the summer of 1951, Belle was "discovered" by a Hollywood agent who saw her at Venice Beach. Belle quickly became a popular character actor who specialized in portraying femme fatales. She ultimately earned enough money to buy a home in Beverly Hills, which Olive enjoys visiting to this day.

Life in America in 1935

Historical Note

"And then the dispossessed were drawn west — from Kansas, Oklahoma, Texas, New Mexico; from Nevada and Arkansas, families, tribes, dusted out, tractored out. Car-loads, caravans, homeless and hungry; twenty thousand and fifty thousand and a hundred thousand and two hundred thousand."

John Steinbeck, *The Grapes of Wrath*

The Dust Bowl represents one of the greatest ecological disasters in the history of our planet. Driven by capitalists' greed and a "sod-busting" attitude that dictated that the natural world was ours to conquer, it was a tragedy equal to the deforestation of China's great river valleys and the current assault on the tropical rain forests of the world. Caught up in the "boom" psychology of the 1920s, the farmers of the plains states sought to maximize profits without regard to the long-term consequences of their actions.

The term *Dust Bowl* was first coined by Associated Press reporter Robert Geiger in April 1935, but the beginnings of the Dust Bowl can be traced to World War I. Until that time most of the grasslands of the southern plains were devoted to grazing. However, as the demand for grain increased in war-ravaged Europe, the lure of profits tempted farmers to plow arid, submarginal land in Nebraska, Kansas, Colorado, Oklahoma, Texas, and New Mexico.

The crop production was good at first, and fortunes were made. Continued speculation after the war accelerated the destruction of the native grasslands. More and more acres were put under cultivation as tractors replaced mules and horses. With the exception of a handful of Native Americans, who warned against the dangers of turning the prairie into farms, few people could foresee the environmental disaster that was waiting to happen.

Farmers got the first hint that all was not well when crop prices fell in the 1920s. Postwar reconstruction had put European farmers back into competition, while at the same time, improvements in tractors, one-way disk plows, and combines allowed American farmers to produce more grain than the markets demanded. Every new tractor put a few more farmhands out of work. Small farmers who couldn't afford to buy the new equipment were "tractored out" and forced to sell their land. Farming had suddenly become a big business that required a large capital investment. To keep up with the huge payments on both land and equipment, farmers were forced to plow up ever larger tracts of land. Yet even as the farms got bigger, profit margins got tighter.

The situation was further complicated by the stock market crash of 1929, which signaled the beginning of the Great Depression. Many farmers couldn't pay their debts. Bank foreclosures and sheriff's auctions became commonplace across the plains as farms were sold to the highest bidder. So few people had cash available that in many cases the creditors were the only bidders to show up at the auctions. Formerly self-sufficient farmers now found themselves unemployed, and in many cases, homeless. Responding to reports that jobs were available on farms in Arizona and California, hundreds of thousands of displaced people headed west in search of work.

As bad as things were on the plains, they were about to get worse. The first sign of an impending ecological disaster came in the summer of 1931. A severe drought hit the Midwestern and southern plains. As the crops died and the soil dried out, dust from overplowed and overgrazed land became airborne, causing what became known as "black blizzards" or "dusters." Over the next few years the drought continued, and the number of dust storms increased rapidly. Fourteen were reported in 1932 and thirty-eight in 1933.

By 1934 75 percent of the country was affected by the drought. On May 11 of that year one of the worst storms on record blew away 300 million tons of topsoil in a single day. Dust clouds darkened the sky as far away as New York and New England, and gritty deposits were found on ships two hundred miles out to sea. The *Yearbook of Agriculture* of 1934 said that "100 million acres now in crops have lost all or most of the topsoil."

The worst storm on record hit on April 14, 1935, a peaceful Palm Sunday afternoon that would become known as "Black Sunday." Cyclonic winds traveling at speeds up to 100 miles per hour rolled out of the Dakotas and traveled quickly across Nebraska, Kansas, eastern Colorado, Oklahoma, Texas, and New Mexico. Dirt clouds churned 20,000 feet into the air and created a thousand-mile-wide "duster." By the end of the day the storm had traveled 1,500 miles and inundated everything in its path.

The "epicenter" of the Dust Bowl was Cimarron County in the Oklahoma Panhandle. The county's wheat crop, which yielded $700,000 in 1930, declined to only $7,000 in 1933, and virtually nothing in 1934. Farmers who had managed to stay in business tried to recoup their losses by plowing even more land under in 1935. This only made the Dust Bowl worse.

Cimarron County experienced a 40 percent population loss during the 1930s. The dispossessed people generally migrated to nearby states, with the more adventuresome heading west to Arizona and California via Route 66 in hope of making new lives for themselves. Though only 20 percent of these forced migrants were from Oklahoma, the term *Okie* was applied to them all.

The journey to California was not an easy one. Single men tended to hitchhike or bum rides on freight trains. Families drove old jalopies and rickety stake-bed trucks, piling what few possessions they could on their vehicles and homemade trailers. The intense heat of the deserts and the steep mountain slopes put a strain on men and machines. Cars overheated and broke down. Road shoulders became cluttered with abandoned cars and discarded belongings.

Once people arrived in California, conditions were just as bad as back home. Unemployment was high, and the waves of fresh migrant workers allowed the large growers to cut wages beyond their already low level. In many towns the new arrivals were greeted by signs that read OKIES GO HOME. Families were forced to live in "ditch bank" camps or in clusters of shacks, often called "Hoovervilles" after President Herbert Hoover. Sanitary conditions were so poor in these camps that diseases such as typhoid, malaria, smallpox, and tuberculosis spread rapidly. Entire families needed to work in the fields to make enough money to survive, and since child labor laws didn't apply to agriculture, children as young as seven and eight endured long days in the hot sun picking cotton and fruit, or weeding the endless rows of vegetables.

No one described the conditions of these migrant workers more vividly than Nobel Prize-winner John Steinbeck. Though his 1939 novel *The Grapes of Wrath* received critical acclaim, the Board of Supervisors of Kern County, California, voted to ban his book shortly after its publication. Farmers even burned copies in the streets. Though the ban was rescinded a few years later, the book was not taught in the local high school until 1972.

Shortly after his inauguration in 1933, Franklin Delano Roosevelt took a number of aggressive steps to energize the failing U.S. economy and to change the agricultural practices that had contributed to the creation of the Dust Bowl. In March 1933 he declared a four-day bank holiday and urged Congress to pass the Emergency Banking Act of 1933. Next he signed the Taylor Grazing Act, establishing grazing districts that would be carefully monitored. Roosevelt also tried to slow farm foreclosures by urging Congress to pass the Emergency Farm Mortgage Act, which allotted $200 million for refinancing farm mortgages. Further help came from the Farm Credit Act.

In the fall of 1933 the price of meat was so low that 6 million young pigs were destroyed in an effort to stabilize prices. Public outcry over this waste led Congress to create the Federal Surplus Relief Corporation. The FSRC gave agricultural commodities such as apples, beans, canned beef, flour, and pork products to relief organizations for local distribution.

Another organization that helped farmers was the Drought Relief Service. The DRS bought cattle in the hardest-hit counties. Those unfit for human consumption were destroyed, and the remaining cattle were given to the Federal Surplus Relief Corporation for use in their food distribution program.

Perhaps the most sweeping legislation of all came in the form of the Emergency Relief Appropriation Act, which provided a total of $525 million for drought relief. It also authorized the establishment of the Works Progress Administration, an agency that would ultimately provide jobs for 8.5 million unemployed people.

Knowing that additional, stronger measures were needed to prevent further soil erosion from destroying valuable cropland, Roosevelt also urged Congress to pass a number of other programs. The newly established Soil Conservation Service in the Department of Agriculture offered incentives to farmers who were willing to employ soil-conserving techniques that included strip cropping, terracing, crop rotation, contour plowing, and the use of cover crops. The SCS also wrote a soil conservation law, which allowed farmers to set up their own local districts to enforce soil conservation practices.

To further protect the land, FDR began a Shelterbelt Project, which called for the large-scale planting of trees across the Great Plains. FDR designated a 100-mile-wide zone from Canada to northern Texas and paid farmers to cultivate trees. By 1938 the use of shelter belts and improved plowing techniques had reduced erosion by 65 percent. However, the drought lingered until the fall of 1939, when rains finally returned. This welcome greening, followed soon after by the boost in demand for food production generated by World War II, brought prosperity back to the plains.

Whether this prosperity continues or not will depend to a great extent on how well we apply the lessons we have learned from the Dust Bowl. Without careful stewardship of the land, Black Sunday could one day return.

Tempted by a wartime boom in wheat profits, farmers over-plowed and overgrazed the grasslands of Colorado, Kansas, Nebraska, New Mexico, Oklahoma, and Texas. With a drought, the soil became so dry that it no longer stayed on the ground—wind blew it up into the air, creating a dust storm. Here, a man and his children run for shelter as a dust storm, also called a "duster," approaches.

The ground was bare in the Dust Bowl region in the 1930s. The once fertile land became arid and coated with layers of loose dirt. Trees lost their leaves, and there were no more pastures in which farm animals could graze. The sky in this region was filled with traces of dust that filled the lungs of humans and animals alike, causing a dangerous and sometimes fatal disease called Dust Pneumonia.

A barn is nearly buried by drifts of dirt that were blown in by a duster in Kansas in 1936. After winds blew around the loose earth, the soil would resettle in wave-like patterns and create great drifts that could cover up homes and other structures.

Thick, black curtains of dirt, the ominous sign of a duster, blow into a town in the Great Plains of the American Middle West.

This family of migrants journeyed in 1938 from Oklahoma to the San Joaquin Valley in California to escape the Dust Bowl. Their car is loaded with all the belongings it could carry. The extreme conditions to which the cars and migrants were exposed made the journey difficult, and sometimes perilous, but the migrants were lured by the promise of a verdant California overflowing with available jobs.

In an attempt to prevent diseased fruits, vegetables, and livestock from getting out of the disaster-stricken Dust Bowl region, policemen inspected migrant cars making the journey to California. Residents also did not welcome the thousands of migrants entering their state, as California's rate of unemployment continued to spiral downward.

Nobel Prize–winning author John Steinbeck vividly described the migrants' experience in his 1939 novel, The Grapes of Wrath. *Steinbeck so perfectly evoked the terrible conditions which the migrants endured that the Board of Supervisors in the California county in which the story was set voted to ban it, and farmers burned copies of the book in the streets.*

Migrant labor camps popped up all over California as waves of people flooded in to escape the Dust Bowl. The Great Depression made conditions quite unfavorable, however. Unemployment was rampant, and the new arrivals were often forced to live in shantytowns, also called Hoovervilles, of tents or tin-roofed shacks. The mud and lack of facilities created terrible conditions, and diseases such as malaria, typhoid, and tuberculosis were widespread. Working conditions were often not any better.

Migrant families in California were often very poor and had to send their children to work in the fields. There were no child labor laws that applied to agricultural work, and so children as young as seven or eight years old could be forced to work long days in the burning sun, harvesting beans, strawberries, cotton, and other crops.

The Arvin Federal Camp, also known as Weedpatch, was the first federally funded migrant camp. The living conditions in the camp were significantly better than in the Hoovervilles, as Weedpatch was run by Tom Collins (pictured in the bottom photograph), who believed in letting the migrants govern themselves. The migrants appointed Child Welfare, Recreation and Entertainment, and Good Neighbor Committees, as well as a Campers' Committee to control discipline and order. The camp was run extraordinarily well, and it even included a clinic and a school.

Migrants traveled along Route 66 until they reached the green hills of California. Attractive posters on the side of the road advertised work opportunities and beautiful scenes of the ocean, palm trees, and lush fields, but upon arrival in California, the migrants learned that there were not enough jobs to go around.

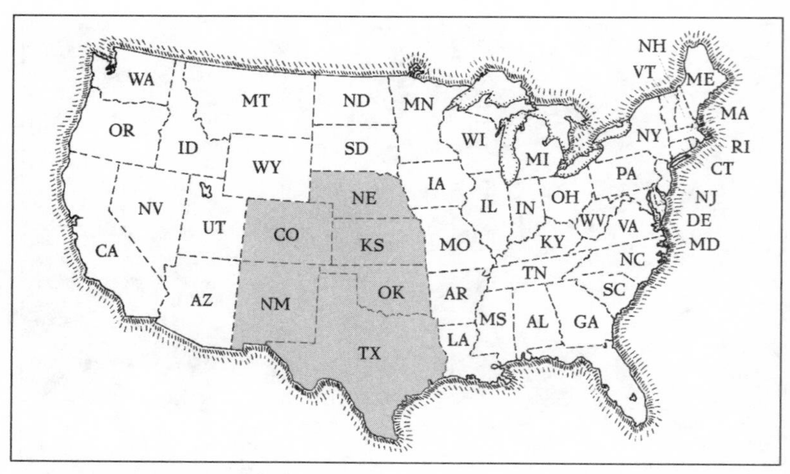

This map shows the continental United States of America. The highlighted states were affected by Dust Bowl.

About the Author

WILLIAM DURBIN is the author of four books of historical fiction: *The Broken Blade, Wintering,* and for the My Name Is America series, *The Journal of Sean Sullivan, A Transcontinental Railroad Worker* and *The Journal of Otto Peltonen, A Finnish Immigrant. The Broken Blade* won the Great Lakes Booksellers Association Award and the Minnesota Book Award. It was named to the New York Public Library's Books for the Teen Age List and was a Bank Street College Children's Book of the Year. In a pointer review, *Kirkus Reviews* said, "Durbin's first novel is an impressive coming-of-age tale set in Montreal at the dawn of the nineteenth century. . . . Readers will embrace this unusual journey and its path to true bravery, strength of character, and self-reliance."

William Durbin says, "Though I have written in a variety of genres including poetry, plays, and essays, historical fiction remains my favorite. Interviewing people and searching through period newspapers, diaries, letters, books, and magazines in an attempt to capture the character of another time is both a challenge and an adventure."

William Durbin has taught on every level from fourth grade to college. He is currently on leave from teaching college composition and high school English. Mr. Durbin has supervised writing research projects for the National Council of Teachers of English and Middlebury College's Bread Loaf School of English. He lives on Lake Vermilion in northern Minnesota, with his wife, Barbara, who also is a teacher. They have a son, Reid, and a daughter, Jessica.

To the many who made this journey,
& to Jean Feiwel and Amy Griffin
for their continued faith in the
intelligence of young readers

Acknowledgments

I would like to thank the people of Oklahoma who were so generous in sharing their knowledge of the history of the plains. These fine folks include Phyllis Randolph of the Cimarron Heritage Center; Norma Gene Young, author of *Black Sunday*; Becky Walker, Boise City assessor; Pat Ramsey and her Boise City eighth-grade class, who compiled *The Dust Bowl Gazette*; C.M. Cole, expert oilman, rancher, Model T owner, and linksman; and the following staff of the Oklahoma Historical Society: Richard Harris, Judith Michner, and Delbert Amen.

In addition, I would like to recognize Robert Parks of the Roosevelt Library; Barbara Mitchell of the Cal State University Library and California Odyssey Project; John Karlick and Hodge Black of the Kern County Agricultural Extension Service; John Walden of the Beale Memorial Library; the reference staffs of the Los Angeles and Santa Monica public libraries; the Natural Toxins Research Center at Texas A&M University, and the Santa Monica-Malibu Unified School District.

As always, the assistance of the Hibbing and Virginia public libraries, the Minnesota Historical Society, and the University of Minnesota Duluth Library has been invaluable.

Finally, my gratitude goes out to my agent, Barbara Markowitz, and to my family, Barbara, Jessica, and Reid, for their many years of encouragement and support.

Grateful acknowledgment is made for permission to reprint the following:

Cover portrait: Photograph by Walker Evans/Farm Security Administration, United States Department of Agriculture, courtesy of the Library of Congress. Negative # LC-USF33-TO1-009012.

Cover background: Photograph by BC McLean/Hulton Archive. Negative #M131435 BOX 9195/4.

Foldout map: Bryn Bernard.

Page 158 (top): Man and children running for shelter: Photograph by Arthur Rothstein/United States Department of Agriculture, Farm Security Administration, Negative #27751.

Page 158 (bottom): Cattle and windmill: Courtesy of the Library of Congress, # LC-USF34-004048-E.

Page 159 (top): Soil drifts: Photograph by Arthur Rothstein/Farm Security Administration, United States Department of Agriculture, courtesy of the Library of Congress.

Page 159 (bottom): "Approaching Dust Storm in Middle West": The Kansas State Historical Society, Topeka, Kansas. ZC.9 STO.D . 1935c *11.

Page 160 (top): "Family on the Road, Midwest": Photograph by Dorothea Lange. Courtesy of the Dorothea Lange Collection, Oakland Museum of California, City of Oakland. Gift of Paul S. Taylor. A67.137.38239.2. c.1938.

Page 160 (bottom): Police inspection: American Stock/Hulton Archive Photos.

Page 161: *The Grapes of Wrath:* Reproduced from the Collections of the Library of Congress.

Page 162 (top): "Coachella Housing": Photograph by Dorothea Lange. Courtesy of the Dorothea Lange Collection, Oakland Museum of California, City of Oakland. Gift of Paul S. Taylor. A67.137.94768. c. 1935.

Page 162 (bottom): Child worker: Photograph by Dorothea Lange/Farm Security Administration, United States Department of Agriculture, courtesy of the Library of Congress, # LC-USF34.

Page 163 (top): "Arvin Camp Settling Down": Photograph by Dorothea Lange. Courtesy of the Dorothea Lange Collection, Oakland Museum of California,City of Oakland, Gift of Paul S. Taylor A67.137.40033.1. c.1940

Page 163 (bottom): "Tom Collins and the Walter Packard Family": Photograph by Dorothea Lange. Courtesy of the Dorothea Lange Collection, Oakland Museum of California, City of Oakland. Gift of Paul S. Taylor. A67.137.35137.1. c. 1935.

Page 164 (top): "Santa Monica 66 End of the Trail": Photograph by Adelbert Bartlett. Courtesy of the Carolyn Farnham Collection, Santa Monica Public Library Archives. c. 1935.

Page 164 (bottom): Map by Heather Saunders.

Other books in the My Name Is America series

The Journal of William Thomas Emerson
A Revolutionary War Patriot
by Barry Denenberg

The Journal of James Edmond Pease
A Civil War Union Soldier
by Jim Murphy

The Journal of Joshua Loper
A Black Cowboy
by Walter Dean Myers

The Journal of Scott Pendleton Collins
A World War II Soldier
by Walter Dean Myers

The Journal of Sean Sullivan
A Transcontinental Railroad Worker
by William Durbin

The Journal of Ben Uchida
Citizen 13559, Mirror Lake Internment Camp
by Barry Denenberg

The Journal of Jasper Jonathan Pierce
A Pilgrim Boy
by Ann Rinaldi

The Journal of Wong Ming-Chung
A Chinese Miner
by Laurence Yep

The Journal of Augustus Pelletier
The Lewis & Clark Expedition
by Kathryn Lasky

The Journal of Otto Peltonen
A Finnish Immigrant
by William Durbin

The Journal of Jesse Smoke
The Trail of Tears
by Joseph Bruchac

The Journal of Biddy Owens
The Negro Leagues
by Walter Dean Myers

The Journal of Douglas Allen Deeds
The Donner Party Expedition
by Rodman Philbrick

The Journal of Patrick Seamus Flaherty
United States Marine Corps
by Ellen Emerson White

While the events described and some of the characters in this book may be based on actual historical events and real people, C.J. Jackson is a fictional character, created by the author, and his journal and its epilogue are works of fiction.

Library of Congress Cataloging-in-Publication Data

Durbin, William, 1951–
The journal of C.J. Jackson : a Dust Bowl migrant / by William Durbin. — 1st ed.
p. cm. — (My Name is America)
Summary: Thirteen-year-old C.J. records in a journal the conditions of the Dust Bowl that cause the Jackson family to leave their farm in Oklahoma and make the difficult journey to California, where they find a harsh life as migrant workers.
ISBN 0-439-15306-9
1. Depressions — 1929 — Juvenile fiction. 2. Dust storms — Oklahoma — Oklahoma Panhandle — Juvenile fiction. [1. Depressions — 1929 — Fiction. 2. Dust storms — Oklahoma — Fiction. 3. Droughts — Oklahoma — History — Fiction. 4. Family life — Fiction. 5. Migrant labor — Fiction. 6. Oklahoma — Fiction. 7. California — Fiction.] I. Title. II. Series.
PZ7.D9323 Jk 2002
[Fic] — dc21 2001041150

10 9 8 7 6 5 4 3 2 1 02 03 04 05 06

The display type was set in Canterbury Old Style.
The text type was set in Berling Roman.
Book design by Elizabeth B. Parisi
Photo research by Zoe Moffitt

Printed in the U.S.A.
First edition, April 2002

AUTO ROAD
ATLAS
OF THE
UNITED STATES
IN
1930
ROUTE
US
66